'Ben?'

'Not now.'

He was dressed only in a towel, his skin reddened from the shower. She guessed he'd been scrubbing it, scrubbing off the blood—and the memories?

She followed him into the bedroom and wrapped her arms around him from behind. 'Talk to me.'

'I can't.'

'Please—'

'Meg—'

His voice broke, and he turned in her arms and anchored her head in his trembling hands and locked his mouth to hers in a kiss so filled with pain and desperation that she had no help but to hold him, to press him against her body, to kiss him back…

Caroline Anderson has the mind of a butterfly. She's been a nurse, a secretary, a teacher, run her own soft-furnishing business and now she's settled on writing. She says, 'I was looking for that elusive something. I finally realised it was variety, and now I have it in abundance. Every book brings new horizons and new friends, and in between books I have learned to be a juggler. My teacher husband John and I have two beautiful and talented daughters, Sarah and Hannah, umpteen pets and several acres of Suffolk that nature tries to reclaim every time we turn our backs!' Caroline also writes for the Mills & Boon® Tender Romance™ series.

HOLDING OUT
FOR A HERO

BY
CAROLINE ANDERSON

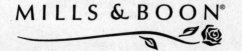

MILLS & BOON®

MILLS & BOON and MILLS & BOON with the Rose Device are registered trademarks of the publisher.

First published in Great Britain 2005
Harlequin Mills & Boon Limited,
Eton House, 18-24 Paradise Road, Richmond, Surrey TW9 1SR

© Caroline Anderson 2005

ISBN 0 263 84321 1

Set in Times Roman 10½ on 12 pt.
03-0805-47221

Printed and bound in Spain
by Litografia Rosés, S.A., Barcelona

CHAPTER ONE

'NO WAY!'

'No way?' Pete Harrison leaned back in his chair, locked his hands behind his head and levelled a thoughtful look at Ben. 'Are you turning into a diva, Maguire?'

His voice was casual, but Ben wasn't fooled for a moment. Casual, nothing. The programme's producer never missed a trick—and every twitching eyelash would be taken down and used in evidence.

Well, he could do casual, too. He crossed one ankle over the opposite knee and picked at a thread on his clean but frankly knackered jeans. He really ought to get some new ones but, dammit, he *liked* these jeans and, anyway, they annoyed Pete, and that in itself made them worth wearing.

He lifted his head and met Pete's eyes head on. 'A diva? After what I've been through for you and your blasted programme? I think that's a tad unjustified,' he said mildly. 'I've been shot at, nearly drowned, I've risked the bends, I've dragged a fireman out of a burning building in the nick of time—I've done everything you've asked of me. I didn't mind, I even enjoyed some of it. But I don't do hospitals—not for you, not for anyone.'

Pete's reply was rude and to the point. 'You're a doctor, for God's sake. Of course you do hospitals.'

'Not any more.'

Pete twiddled his pen with apparent idleness. 'You

5

never did tell me why you gave up medicine,' he said, and Ben felt his muscles tighten.

'No, I didn't,' he said flatly. He wasn't opening that particular can of worms—either now or any time soon—and he had no intention of spending the next week in an A and E department either, good television or not.

As if he realised that line would get him nowhere, Pete put the pen down and leant forwards, changing tack. 'It's the last one of the series,' he said encouragingly. 'We want to end on a high note with a bit of touchy-feely. It's nothing too cutting edge—it's in a nice quiet rural town in the depths of Suffolk, a sleepy little country hospital. Look on it as a holiday.'

Ben snorted rudely. 'Hardly.'

'Ah, come on, Ben. Compared to the lifeboats and the fire service and the deep-sea diving off the oil rigs, it'll be a walk in the park—and light years from a war correspondent. This is a little nurse you're shadowing, that's all. Watching her do her job. Nothing dangerous, nothing threatening.'

That's all you know, Ben thought, but he said nothing, and not by a flicker of those carefully watched eyelashes did he give away the emotion that was roiling inside.

'No.'

Pete's voice was as smooth as polished steel, and with about as much give in it. 'Fly-on-the-wall hospital stuff is hot news at the moment. Blood and guts, heartwrenching drama, the buzz of lives saved—it's what your adoring public want, and let's be clear here, Ben. You give them what they want. It's in your contract.'

The bottom line.

He'd known it was coming. He opened his mouth to

say stuff the contract, but then shut it. He couldn't just walk away midseries, they'd seen to that. *Unsung Heroes* was hugely popular, and he didn't suffer from false modesty. A brilliant idea, it nevertheless owed its success almost entirely to the way he'd flung himself headlong—literally—into the making of every pro-gramme, and they weren't going to let the gravy train hit the buffers because he had a hissy fit.

And anyway, a legal battle to break the contract would be much messier, much harder—much more in-trusive—than just taking a huge deep breath and getting through it.

Somehow.

You can handle it, he told himself. It was years ago—finished. Time to move on, time to let go.

He took that huge deep breath. 'So—who's this little nurse I'm supposed to be shadowing in this sleepy little country hospital?' he asked, and Pete dropped the pen and smiled at him like a friendly barracuda.

'That's my boy,' he said softly. 'I knew you'd see sense.'

'Me? No way!'

'Meg, don't be daft! You'll be wonderful! Everyone loves you—all that bounce and empathy and good-natured teasing, not to mention the high cheekbones and twinkly eyes! You'll be a natural.'

'Angie, I can't!' she wailed at her boss. 'Dream on! This is me—Meg Fraser. I'm not an unsung hero! I'm not any kind of a hero, I'm just a nurse! Who on earth will want to know how I spend my life? I'm a nobody! He does fire-fighters and war correspondents, not boring nurses! Who suggested me, anyway, of all people?'

'I did.'

She spun round and rolled her eyes—her *twinkly* eyes, no less!—at Tom Whittaker, A and E consultant and her best friend's husband. 'I might have known,' she groaned. 'And did Fliss have anything to do with it?'

'She might have done,' he agreed with a lazy smile. 'And don't let her hear you describing nurses as boring. She'll have your guts for garters.'

'If I don't have hers first,' Meg muttered. 'I can't believe you've done this to me! And he'll probably faint at the first sign of blood.'

'Hardly. Ben's a doctor—a good one. He trained with me—we were friends.'

That intrigued her. 'Ben Maguire's a doctor? I thought he was just a pretty face with a death wish. Why did he give up medicine?'

'I have no idea. I'll ask him on Sunday.'

'Sunday?'

'When the team arrives,' Angie chipped in.

'Team?'

'You're beginning to sound like a parrot,' Tom teased. 'The film crew. You know—the cameramen, the sound men, the lighting…'

'*Sunday?*' Meg shrieked. 'They can't start on Sunday!'

'They're starting on Monday,' Angie told her. 'I would have told you all about it, but you were on holiday.'

'You could have sent me a text.'

'What, and risk you not coming back? Where was it? Corfu? Cyprus?'

'Crete,' Meg said mechanically. 'You're right. I might have been forced to miss the plane. Oh, *damn*, I can't believe you've all done this to me!'

'Don't be daft,' Angie said bracingly. 'You'll be great. And you get tomorrow off to sort yourself out— get your uniform sorted, have your hair cut and all that sort of thing, ready for the camera. Still, don't get star-struck just yet. I need someone on Triage right now.'

'No, you need your bumps felt,' Meg said sourly, and with a shake of her head she walked briskly off, mut-tering 'Sunday. *Sunday!*' under her breath.

Behind her, Angie and Tom shared a sigh of relief. She didn't hear it, but she heard the chuckles that fol-lowed, and she could have screamed.

Damn. *Damn!* If she had a grain of sense she'd walk out right this minute.

'Look on the bright side,' Fliss said later when she rang her. 'You won't have to worry about what to wear.'

'No, I'll just look hideous in my uniform!'

'You don't look hideous in anything. Don't be silly. You're gorgeous—all lush curves like Kate Winslet.'

'I'd rather look like Cameron Diaz—all eyes and no lush at all.'

'How about looking like Meg Fraser? At least you've *got* a waist, unlike some of us.'

'Do I get a choice?' Meg said drily, then sighed. 'Oh, well, I know one person who'll be pleased. My mother will die of excitement. She loves the programme and she thinks Ben Maguire's gorgeous.'

'And you don't?' Fliss teased. 'Come on—six feet of solid testosterone with those wicked, amazing eyes and that sexy grin—lord, girl, if I wasn't married…'

'Well, you are, and Tom's no slouch and he loves you to bits, not that you deserve it. Just thank your lucky stars.'

'I do. Every day,' Fliss said gently. 'He's wonderful

and I love him to bits, too. And I won't be distracted. We were talking about you.'

'And you should be talking about whether or not I'll forgive you for setting me up,' Meg pointed out, not at all sure that she would.

'Of course you will. You'll have a great time, and it's only for a few days, anyway.'

A few days? Well, it probably was, but it seemed huge to her then, just three days away from the start of it all. And her hair was a mess, trashed by a week on the beach in Crete, and her nose was peeling, and she'd be on television.

Television, for heaven's sake! Never mind the hair and the nose, she could get them sorted tomorrow, but what about her mouth? Given the slightest provocation she'd say something stupid for sure, and it would come back to haunt her, in the way of these things, for years to come.

'I don't think I *will* forgive you,' she said to Fliss. 'With my ability to run off at the mouth I could ruin my career and probably his, too, with a few carefully un-chosen words!'

Fliss laughed. 'Rubbish. You're lovely, they'll adore you and it would take dynamite to ruin Ben Maguire's career. Anyway, it's not live so they'll edit out the bad bits.'

'You reckon? I hope you're right. And, of course, word will get out and the department will be flooded with drama queens who want to be on the telly. It's OK for you, tucked up safely at home with the children, you don't have to be here to deal with it.' She thought of Fliss's life now, filled with the love and laughter and chaos of a big extended family, and for the briefest moment she felt a little twinge of envy.

Not that she wanted it for herself—heavens, no! But sometimes... 'How's Charlotte?' she asked.

'Gorgeous. I can't believe that at only seven months she's into everything. I can't take my eyes off her for a second. You need to exert a little influence over your god-daughter, teach her how to behave. How about supper on Sunday?'

'What, to bolster me up before the big day?' she said wryly. 'What time?'

'Six? I'll feed the kids early, then you can help me put them to bed and we can settle down with a glass of wine while we knock ourselves up something a bit more sophisticated than fish fingers to eat. How about a barbeque if the weather's nice? With steak and hot chilli chicken and not a burger in sight?'

'Sounds good,' she said, and then remembered she would, by then, have met the great man himself. Oh, rats. How could they all have done this to her?

Ben turned off the car engine and sat for a moment, staring at the hospital as if by some sheer effort of will he might make it go away, but it stayed stubbornly there, right in front of him.

ACCIDENT AND EMERGENCY, it said in huge letters across the front of the ambulance canopy. His worst nightmare come home to roost.

Damn.

And as for it being a sleepy little country hospital— hah! It was a big, sprawling district-general hospital with a real-life full-on A and E department, and any illusions he'd been cherishing about it being otherwise went right out of the window. He pressed his lips together, took a deep breath to waste another second or so and opened the door.

The hospital wasn't going to go away, so he might just as well get on with it. It was an hour before the rest of the team were due to arrive, and he just wanted to do this bit alone, to get inside, to get his reaction over with, to learn in private just how hard it was going to be to go back.

Not that it was the same hospital, but it might as well have been for all the difference it would make.

'You're a fool, forget it,' he told himself, impatient with the dread that lay in a cold lump at the bottom of his stomach. Shrugging it off, he straightened his shoulders, locked the car and strode towards the entrance.

The doors hissed open to let him in, and instantly the smells, the sounds—beeps and groans and fast footfalls, the television in the waiting area, the hushed voices of the patients—assailed his senses and dragged him right back to square one. A child was crying, and in the distance he could hear the rhythmic hiss of a ventilator. He felt his pulse pick up and rammed his hands into his pockets to stop them shaking.

Hell, how could it be so hard?

He stood there, letting it all sink in, his eyes scanning the waiting area and finding familiarities amongst the differences, concentrating on the mundane to distract him from dwelling on the past. The same kinds of posters, the same flickering LED on the electronic message banner announcing the horrendous waiting time—that was something that didn't change, no matter which hospital you were in. They were all the same under the skin.

Unfortunately. He'd hoped it would feel different, but he didn't get that lucky.

He switched his attention to the reception desk just as the receptionist glanced up, did a mild double-take and went pink and girly on him. Dammit, she must have been fifty-five if she was a day, but just the sight of him flustered her, and for once his legendary charm and charisma deserted him.

She leapt up. 'Mr Maguire—I'll call Mr Whittaker for you.'

'No need.' A firm hand landed on his shoulder, and he turned and stared straight into a pair of strangely familiar, smiling eyes.

'Tom?'

Before Ben could react further, he found himself enveloped in a hard, brief hug. Then he was thrust away and scrutinised briefly, then wrapped in another bone-cracking bear hug that brought a lump to his throat. He couldn't remember when anyone had last hugged him with genuine affection, and he found his arms coming up and hugging back, just briefly—just enough. Then he made himself let go, before he blubbed like a baby.

'Damn, I've missed you, you old reprobate,' Tom said gruffly, giving him a hearty slap on the back. He slung an arm around his shoulders and steered him away from Reception. 'Come on, let's get out of here and go somewhere less public. I've nicked Matt Jordan's office, we'll go in there.'

'What on earth are you doing here?' Ben asked, totally confused now. 'How did you know I'd be here?'

'Because I work here—in the department. Been here a year.'

And just like that, any hope of pretending ignorance of medical matters and keeping firmly in the background, pleading squeamishness, went straight down the pan, taking with it any chance of keeping himself to himself.

Tom had been a good friend—a really good friend.

They'd lost touch when their careers had taken them to opposite ends of the country, but no doubt Tom would make it his responsibility to ensure that everything for this shoot ran smoothly, and that was bound to throw them together.

And that, of course, would mean all the inevitable questions about what he'd done since they'd last met, and why he'd given up medicine—and Tom wouldn't be put off with feeble excuses. He'd demand the truth, the whole truth and nothing but the truth, and their friendship deserved honest answers. But he couldn't tell him, couldn't go there, not even for Tom.

Maybe especially for Tom.

And so he'd have to lie, to someone who deserved better and who, of all people, would understand and sympathise, and that, of course, was the trouble. For two pins he'd turn on his heel and run like hell, but he was stuck, because of Pete Harrison and his blasted contract, and there was no way out.

A bad day suddenly got a whole lot worse.

'He's here,' Angie told her, and Meg felt her pulse rate rocket. Damn. She wiped her free hand on her tunic and closed her eyes, tipping her head back and counting to ten. Then fifteen. Then—

'Just go and get it over with. He's in Matt's office with Tom Whittaker. Go on, he won't bite.'

'No, but I might,' Meg said drily. 'Can you manage here?'

'Oh, I think an experienced plaster technician like Max and a senior nursing sister might be just about able to get a cast on a three-year-old,' her superior said with a wry grin, and took the unhappy toddler from her arms.

'Come on, my lovely, you come with Aunty Angie and we'll sort your arm out.'

'Want Meg!' he wailed, and reached for her, but Angie shooed her out, ignoring her reluctance and Adam's tragic wails. Meg blew the little one a kiss for courage and went, via the ladies' loo for a flick of lippie and a quick spritz with the cold tap on her suddenly warm cheeks.

Miraculously her hair was still tidy, but she ran her hand over it critically anyway. Drenching it in conditioner had rescued it and restored the shine, and the mangled ends had been chopped off on Friday, which had made a huge difference. It wasn't great, but at least it didn't look like last year's haystack any longer.

Good enough, she thought critically, and if it wasn't, maybe he'd have someone else from the department. Probably a blonde, not a mousy brunette like her. There were plenty to choose from.

'If I get lucky,' she said with very little hope.

She blew herself a kiss, because like little Adam she needed courage, too, then forced a grin and marched up to Matt's door. Her knuckles had scarcely grazed it when it swung inwards, and there he was, the man himself, right in front of her, propped up on the edge of Matt's desk, and the things his long legs were doing to a pair of faded, worn denim jeans should have been outlawed. She dragged her eyes upwards and stopped in her tracks.

Grief.

She swallowed and tried to remember what she was supposed to be saying and doing, but her mind had inconveniently emptied itself of anything intelligent or relevant and she simply stood there and stared.

Lord, he was gorgeous. So different in real life—what

a cliché, but he was, he really was. Bigger, tougher, more vital, with his chin roughened by stubble and his hair rumpled, a soft mid-brown touched with gold, and his eyes like a wild storm tracking over her, their expression crackling with curiosity and something else, something that drained her of common sense, riveting her to the spot until Tom rescued her.

'Meg, I was just coming to find you,' he said, and, taking her arm, he removed her from the doorway and closed the door behind her. 'Meet an old friend of mine. Ben, this is Sister Megan Fraser, known to all as Meg. Meg, this is—'

The man stuck his hand out. 'Ben Maguire,' he said unnecessarily, and she found her hand enveloped in a firm, brisk handshake that sent shock waves through her system. Still, at least it freed her from her trance, and she conjured up a smile.

'Hi. Good to meet you.' She floundered for something intelligent to say and came up with nothing, so she just smiled again and went for autopilot. 'I gather we're stuck with each other for the week.'

One eyebrow arched above a stormy grey eye, and his mouth twitched.

'I'm sure we'll both survive,' he said drily.

And she thought, So much for my navigation system!

She groaned and shook her head. 'I'm sorry, I didn't mean it to come out like that. I was just—'

'Press-ganged, I believe is the expression,' Tom put in with a grin. Well, at least he hadn't said star-struck, which was nearer to the humiliating truth! But then he went on, 'Poor Meg. She knew nothing about this until Thursday. We set her up while she was sprawled topless on the sand in Crete.'

Ben's eyes dropped automatically to the level of her

chest, and Meg felt her temper fray. Star struck be damned. He was just a man like all the rest. Lifting her hand to the level of her breasts, she raised it slowly until it was just below her eyes, dragging his eyes up with it.

'Thank you,' she said curtly.

A decent man would have been ashamed. Not Ben Maguire. He just studied her in silence for a second, then his mouth quirked.

'My pleasure,' he murmured.

'Ben, behave,' Tom said easily.

'Sorry. I wouldn't like to embarrass her,' Ben replied, his eyes still locked with Meg's, and she raised an incredulous eyebrow. His lips twitched again, and she felt hers firm into a tight line. Tom just snorted.

'No chance. She's made of sterner stuff than that. You wait till you see her deal with the drunks on a Friday night. Our Meg doesn't embarrass easily.'

That's all you know, she thought, and contemplated killing him, but she was saved the effort. His bleep squawked, and with a muttered oath he excused himself. 'Back in a moment, just got to sort something out. I won't be long. Entertain yourselves—I'm sure you'll find something to talk about for a minute or two.'

Yeah, Meg thought, starting with that smart remark and moving on swiftly to some ground rules!

She wasn't wrong. Ben propped himself back on the edge of the desk, folded his arms and gave her a crooked, questioning smile. 'So, were you? Topless?'

She was going to deny it, which was only the truth, but then perversely pride came to her rescue. There was no way she was going to admit to the sexiest man she'd met in ages—no, make that a lifetime—that she'd been the only one on the beach under fifty with a top on! And so she avoided the issue.

'Is it relevant?' she retorted, and he chuckled.

'Not to the programme, no,' he agreed. 'But if I'm going to get to know you…'

His unspoken words hung in the air between them, and Meg found her breath catching as she waited for him to finish the sentence. He didn't, though. Storm-grey gaze still tangling with hers, he lifted one shoulder and smiled. His shrug was Gallic and expressive and deeply sexy, and completely trashed her defences.

She yanked in a deep breath and straightened her shoulders like a prim little miss. 'I don't think you need to get to know me that well,' she said, sounding like an old maid and silently cursing Tom for causing such havoc. Dammit, she wasn't going to fall under this man's spell! She wouldn't! But the silence stretched out between them, humming with tension, and she was wondering what on earth she could say to him next when there was a tap at the door and Sophie appeared with Adam in her arms, sobbing uncontrollably.

'I'm really, really sorry, Meg, but the plaster technician's been called up to the ward and Angie's with Tom and I haven't been trained to apply casts,' she said, as Adam, catching sight of Meg, lunged out of Sophie's arms and threw himself at her.

She fielded him with all the ease of long practice and settled the fractious youngster on her hip, his broken arm carefully cradled between them. 'What's all this, eh? Great big tears! Never mind. Shall we go and get a smart new cast on your arm and then everybody can write on it and draw some new pictures for you—OK?'

Adam hiccuped and cuddled into her, his screams subsiding to a whimper, and she turned to Ben. 'I'm sorry about this,' she said, not at all sorry with this instant escape route from a conversation that had been moving altogether too fast downhill. 'It's his second cast and he's really not keen. I won't be long.'

He shrugged away from the desk. 'Why don't I come with you? I can see the department and get the feel for how you work. Adam won't mind a spectator, will you, mate?'

Damn. Still, he had a point, and she couldn't just leave him there.

Only a week, she told herself. It's only a week.

'OK.'

She didn't wait for his reaction, just headed for the door. He was supposed to be shadowing her. Fine. Let him shadow her, but right now she had a job to do, and Adam came first. If he wanted to watch, he could follow her. That's what shadows did best.

CHAPTER TWO

HE FOLLOWED her.

Ben knew Meg was reluctant, that she'd wanted to get away, but he wasn't prepared to let her slip off that easily. She was gorgeous—fascinating, sexy, and she blushed! Hell, he couldn't remember the last time he'd seen a woman blush about something so simple, and that trick with the hand—that was clever.

And sexy as hell.

And she never had answered the question...

Core business, he told himself, and studied her critically as they walked along the corridor.

She was short—not too short, but a good eight inches or so shorter than him, and he could have tucked her easily under his chin. Resisting the urge to try, he'd taken the firm, capable hand she'd offered him, looked into her challenging blue eyes and been lost.

The camera would love her. The camera, the public—she'd be a real hit. He could just picture it, he thought, assessing her now with the child on her hip. Florence Nightingale with sex appeal. Brilliant.

And she'd been coerced into it. Funny, that—and he knew just how she felt. Although if he had to do it, and Pete had made it very clear that he did, then working with Meg would at least make it bearable.

Well, in one way, at least. In another way it was going to be hard. Very hard. Permanently hard. Thank God his tatty old jeans were tight enough to keep his reaction under control, and his rebelliously untucked shirt was long enough to conceal any give-away bulges.

He sighed quietly and ran his eyes over her again. Soft, womanly curves, not fat but not in the slightest bit boyish. Oh, no. This one was all woman, and a woman, he sensed, with personality to burn.

He wondered if she *had* been topless on the beach. So what? He usually thought nothing of it. Everyone did it these days, it was nothing remarkable.

But the very thought of Meg on a beach wearing nothing but a slick of oil and a pair of skimpy briefs had been enough to bring him to his knees, and he'd still been struggling with the image when the door had opened and a saint in the guise of a young staff nurse had rescued him before he'd embarrassed himself.

Trailing Meg down the corridor now, he watched as she cradled the little boy against her chest and soothed him with her gentle, singsong voice, and he realised that she was a wonderful choice.

Thank God, she'll carry the programme, he thought, so I won't have to, and he was just beginning to think that it would all be fine when the child looked at him over her shoulder, his eyes huge and solemn and tear-stained, and he felt as if he'd been kicked in the solar plexus.

He's just a child. There are millions of them in the world. Get over it, he told himself fiercely, and then Meg glanced back and gave him a curious look. She was saying something about the history of Adam's fracture, telling him what she was going to do.

Nothing drastic, nothing radical—just a routine procedure on a little boy like any other, with huge wet eyes and a gut-wrenching wobble to his little rosebud mouth that could break a man's heart. Telling himself he was being ridiculous, he forced his legs to carry on walking, catching up with her, opening the door for her while she carried Adam into the plaster room.

They'd lost Sophie *en route*, called away to another patient, and so it was just the three of them. No big deal. He only had to watch and talk to her while she did this simple procedure. How hard could it be?

Very, was the answer, and for reasons that caught him totally unawares. Nothing to do with the hospital and the dread that lurked in the pit of his stomach, or his unexpected and rather troubling reaction to Meg, and everything to do with those great wet eyes and a totally unexpected feeling of homesickness.

He wanted to help. Wanted to take the child into his arms and make him smile, and soothe his fears, but that was ridiculous. And it terrified him. He propped himself up against the wall of the plaster room and asked stupid questions instead, his arms firmly folded.

'So where's Mum?'

'Gone for a cup of tea and a sit-down—she's preg-nant again and her blood pressure's a bit high, so we told her to go and take it easy. We thought we could cope without her. Seems we were wrong. Adam, do you want to sing a song while we put your new cast on?'

Adam shook his head and buried his face in her shoulder. 'Don't want new cast,' he mumbled tearfully. 'Want old cast.'

'You can keep it, Adam, you just can't wear it any more, darling, because it's too sloppy on your arm now. He had a backslab at first,' she explained to Ben, 'then the other cast, but once the swelling went down he could take his arm right out of it. It was quite a nasty fracture and it just needs another week or so of support, but it'll have to be a new one.'

'Want my old one,' he sobbed, and Ben's heart twisted all over again.

'Why so attached?' he asked, struggling for something sensible to say.

'Because everybody's drawn on it. He likes the pictures on the other one.'

Sucked in despite himself, he shrugged away from the wall. 'May I see?'

'Of course. It's there.'

He picked it up, turned it in his hands, studied the colourful doodles and scrawls that covered the little green resin cast. So small. Such a tiny arm. 'It's a bit full,' he said, hunkering down by Adam's side. 'You could have more pictures on the new one, then you'd have two. You could keep them both, then,' he said.

Adam lifted his head and studied Ben dubiously with those huge eyes. 'You draw pictures for me?'

'Sure, if you want.'

He sniffed and rubbed his nose on his hand, and Meg found him a tissue and mopped him up.

'So will you let me put the new cast on now?' she asked, and he nodded, his lip wobbling again.

'You'll have to hold him,' she said, and Ben jack-knifed up and backed away.

'I can't,' he said flatly, but Meg tipped her head on one side and looked at him as if he'd lost his marbles.

'Don't be ridiculous,' she said briskly. 'You're a doctor—of course you can hold him.'

And just like that, without warning, he found his arms full of small boy. Small, warm, wriggling boy, snuggling into his chest. He looked down and encountered wide, wet eyes and a doubtful mouth, and his heart twisted.

'Well, hi, there,' he said with a grin that he could feel was crooked. God, it had been so long…

'Sit here,' Meg instructed, indicating a chair at the end of the work table. He manoeuvred himself onto the chair with the warm little body on his lap, and Meg crouched down in front of him and smiled reassuringly at Adam.

'Right, tiger, what colour would you like this time? You can have red, blue or green.'

'B'ue.'

'OK, blue it is. Can you remember what we do first?'

'F'uffy stuff,' Adam said, and Meg nodded and ruffled his hair.

'Good man! Fluffy stuff first, all over your arm where the cast will go, then I'm going to wrap it all up in the wet bandage. And then, when it's all dry and set, Ben can draw on it for you. Just remember, we mustn't touch it until it sets, or we'll stick to it, OK? So I'll have gloves on, and you must keep very, very still for me so we don't get in a mess.'

Adam nodded, his little head bobbling solemnly against Ben's chest, and while Ben supported his elbow, Meg wrapped the little arm in wadding and then swathed it quickly in the wet cast bandage, her hands winding it deftly round and round over the wadding to make a firm support for the tiny arm.

'Very neat. Anybody would think you'd done that before,' he murmured, striving for a neutral topic, and she tipped her head back and grinned.

'Once or twice. We have a team of technicians who normally do all this sort of thing,' she told him as she smoothed and snipped, 'but we can do the simple casts if we have to, and sometimes it's better—keeps the number of people handling the child down to a minimum, which is good. Right, sport, all done, and we didn't get any on us!'

A few minutes with the hair-dryer, and Meg sat back to admire her handiwork.

'Good. That's great. And now you'll have two lots of pictures, won't you?' she said, smiling at the little boy.

Adam nodded slowly, his head resting against Ben's chest and bringing back a surge of memories.

He shut them down.

'So what are we going to draw on this one, Adam?'

'Twain,' Adam demanded, and Ben chuckled, the laughter hitching in his throat as the little boy looked up at him and grinned.

Hell, he'd missed those trusting smiles…

No. Draw a train, he told himself, and stick to the present.

Except, of course, he'd reckoned without Meg.

'Tom told me you were at med school with him,' she said conversationally a few minutes later as she waved Adam out of the door, cast duly decorated and Mum back in charge. 'Bit of a career change, isn't it?'

It was pointless denying it, so he simply nodded. 'It was a long time ago.'

Lifetimes.

Straightening his shoulders, he looked past her to see a familiar vehicle coming into view in the car park. 'Looks like the team are here,' he said in relief, and set off to meet them.

Never had the cavalry been more welcome.

'So, tell me, what's he like?'

Meg patted the dog who'd come to greet her and sauntered across the grass towards her friend, sprawled in the shade under a huge copper beech. 'Getting right to the point, aren't you?' she grinned. 'Have you been in suspense, petal?'

'As if you wouldn't have been,' Fliss said with a chuckle. 'So? Come on, let's hear all about it. How is he, up close and personal?'

Meg sighed and flopped down on the rug next to Fliss, the dog following suit. 'Gorgeous,' she said honestly. 'I knew he would be, he's a real heartbreaker, you can tell that from the programmes, but up close and personal—wow. Pity he's a womanising bastard.'

'He is?'

Meg rolled her eyes. 'Oh, yes. He couldn't take his eyes off my chest—and that was Tom's fault, talking about me sunbathing topless in Crete.'

Fliss's eyes widened. 'He said what? I'll kill him.'

'Get in the queue,' Meg advised her. 'Believe me, it wasn't the best start.'

'How did he know you were?'

'Were what? Topless? He didn't. I didn't! Of course I didn't do it! You know I hate my chest. There's no way I'm getting it out in public. And he ogled me.'

'*Tom?*' Fliss shrieked.

'No, Ben,' Meg said hastily before she had a divorce on her hands. 'Tom wouldn't do that, he doesn't even know I'm a woman. Ben ogled. And grinned, dammit, with that sexy almost-grin. I could have slapped him.'

Fliss started to laugh, and Meg punched her arm lightly.

'What? *What?*'

'You. You're so sarcastic about men all the time, so dismissive, and you've spent an hour or so with this guy and you're in love!'

'I'm not in love!' Meg denied vehemently. 'Weren't you listening to a word I just said?'

'Like "gorgeous" and "wow" and "heartbreaker", for instance? And "sexy almost-grin", even?'

'Well, it is, and he is a heartbreaker—just not *my* heart. No way, but that doesn't make me blind. I just think he's a sexy-looking guy. Very sexy, but unfortunately he knows it. And, infuriatingly, he can be nice when he's not being a womanising bastard. You should have seen him with one of the little kids—he was wonderful. I wonder which branch of medicine he was in and why he gave up?'

Fliss shrugged. 'Dunno. Tom doesn't know either. I'm surprised you didn't ask him, though. It's not like you to hold back, you're usually straight in there.'

Meg shook her head, for once not responding to Fliss's mild teasing. It was true, she was pretty direct usually, but...

'I did ask, sort of—well, gave him a chance to talk,' she said thoughtfully. 'He didn't take it. There was just something about him, though—something untouchable. He didn't say anything, but once or twice I caught him looking at little Adam and there was something in his eyes. I did mention that I knew he'd trained with Tom, sort of casually, but he just said "it was a long time ago" in a really hands-off kind of way, and I couldn't pursue it after that, but...'

'Oh, hell, he's in for it. You're lethal when you're curious.'

She shook her head. Oddly, she didn't feel curious, more...concerned. 'I think something happened,' she said slowly. 'Something momentous that made him give up.'

'There's usually a trigger for a lifestyle change,' Fliss

pointed out pragmatically. 'I shouldn't read too much into it. Loads of doctors give up, they just can't hack it after a while. I expect Tom can get it out of him. They used to be really close friends, I gather, but they drifted apart. I don't think Jane liked him very much.'

'Perhaps he couldn't stop looking at her chest either?' Meg suggested, but Fliss shook her head.

'Tom doesn't know what happened, but something did, and reading between the lines I think it's more likely it was Jane at fault. Right, I need to get this lot rounded up and into bed. Want to bath Charlotte? She's inside with her grandparents, because she's been crawling around on the grass all day and her little legs are a bit pink.'

'Grass rash?'

'Probably. A nice lavender-oil bath should settle it down, and I know how you love getting splashed.'

And cuddling her little god-daughter, Meg thought, but she kept it to herself. She wasn't really broody, but if Fliss got the slightest hint of it she'd be matchmaking like crazy, and Fliss with the bit between her teeth was a terrifying prospect. Still, at least this Ben Maguire thing would keep her occupied for a week, and there was no way even Fliss would try and matchmake *that* combination, surely! Not after what she'd said about him.

She got to her feet. 'You're just trying to get a free nanny for the evening,' she said drily.

'Rumbled,' Fliss said with a laugh, and Meg helped her coax Michael and Abby out of the tree house Tom had built for them in the branches overhead.

'I'll read you a bedtime story if you come now,' she wheedled, and Michael promptly outsmarted her.

'Three chapters,' he said, and she sighed.

'Two,' she compromised, and they came down and ran inside, giggling and shrieking and still full of it, the dog bounding at their heels.

'I don't know where they get their energy,' Fliss said, shaking her head. 'And I don't know why you're reading to them, they're quite capable of reading to themselves. They're six now, nearly seven.'

'Because bedtime stories are lovely,' Meg said. 'And anyway, I know you do it, too.'

Fliss chuckled. 'Yes, and I'm deeply grateful to you for taking it over, but—two chapters? Sucker,' she sang, and Meg laughed.

'Very likely, but I read fast.'

'Just so long as you aren't up there for hours, because I've told Tom to bring Ben back here for supper—'

'What?' Meg wailed, horrified. 'I look a total mess! I'm dressed for bathing the kids and chilling out, and you tell me now the sexiest man I've ever met is coming for supper? I hate you!'

Fliss laughed. 'No, you don't, you love me really. And you look fine. Anyway, I thought you weren't interested?'

'I still don't need to look like a bag lady,' she said in exasperation, ready to kill her friend for the second time in a few short days. 'Dear God, you owe me, Fliss Ryman—big time.'

'Whittaker—and get over it. Who knows? I could be doing you a favour.'

Somehow Meg didn't think so, and she had a horrible sinking feeling that she and Ben weren't, after all, going to be safe from Fliss's matchmaking.

She thought of the expression in his eyes when he'd asked her about being topless, and she felt heat scorch her cheeks.

And, of course, Fliss saw.

'Thought so,' she said, and Meg could have smacked her.

'It's hot,' she said, but Fliss just smiled knowingly, and Meg gave up.

'OK, guys, thanks a lot. I'll see you in the morning, bright and early. Meg's shift starts at seven, so six sharp should do it. Don't be late.'

The team grumbled off towards the van that was parked on the fringe of the car park, and Pete turned to Ben with a look in his eye that boded trouble.

'That goes double for you, Maguire,' the producer warned, and Ben rolled his eyes.

'When am I ever late?' he asked, and Pete snorted.

'Never—but you give us all fits and there's always a first time. Just be here early, hmm? Five to instead of five past would be good. And for pity's sake ditch the poverty image. You're getting scruffier by the minute. Heaven knows, we pay you enough, it's not as if you can't afford clothes.'

'Don't worry, I've packed my party frock,' Ben retorted, letting sarcasm get the better of him for once. But he was getting tired of Pete's little digs. OK, so he was a bit of a loose cannon off set, but he was always on time, he dressed appropriately for the camera, he ticked all the right boxes. There was no need for Pete's attitude, and he was frankly sick of it.

Pete opened his mouth, took another look at Ben's face and shut it. 'Fine. I'll see you in the morning.' He lifted a hand in farewell as he strolled off, and slowly, reluctantly, Ben turned to Tom, knowing what was coming and with his arguments all ready.

'So what are your plans for the evening?' Tom asked,

right on cue. 'In fact, whatever they are, cancel them. I've got instructions and if I don't take you home my life won't be worth living.'

Ben shook his head. 'I need to sort out a few things with the team for the morning and then get an early night,' he said, deeply reluctant to spend an evening in Jane's company, but Tom just raised a sceptical eyebrow.

'Early night? This is me you're talking to. I know you can get by on three hours' sleep, I've seen you do it—been there while you did. And the arrangements for the morning are all set up, so that won't wash. What the hell is it? A hot date?'

He might have known Tom wouldn't take it lying down. He sighed inwardly. 'No hot date.'

'Your wife, then.'

'Not married,' he said economically, definitely not getting into that one.

'So you've got no damned excuse at all, have you? And if you don't come I'll be in deep doo-doo. Felicity won't forgive me,' he said, and despite himself Ben's curiosity was piqued.

'Felicity?' his mouth said before he could stop it, and that was it, a chink in the armour, and Tom was right in there.

'My wife. You'll like her.'

'What happened to Jane?'

Damn, he hadn't meant to ask, hadn't meant to allow Tom to draw him into this sort of personal conversation, but at least it diverted attention the other way, away from him, and that had to be good.

'She walked out about four or five years ago—left me with four kids and went off to Germany with her lover.'

'Ouch.' Ben winced, but Tom was smiling.

'Best thing she could have done for all of us, although it didn't feel like that at the time. Felicity's wonderful—but she's a formidable woman when she's crossed, and she's expecting you, so if you've got any kindness left in you, you'll spare me!'

Damn. He really, really didn't want to do this, but Tom had been a good friend, and without being appallingly rude there was no way out. As if he sensed his impending capitulation, Tom clamped a hand on his shoulder and grinned. 'Good man. Where's your car? You can follow me.'

And just like that, he was cut off at the pass. With a sigh of resignation, he got into his car and followed Tom. They drove out of town for a few minutes, and then he turned in between old red-brick gateposts and round a sweeping gravel drive and pulled up outside the front of a house.

A gorgeous house—mellow red brick, early Victorian, he guessed, but it could have been older, and it was in immaculate order. Immaculate, that was, except for the abundant evidence of family life—a small pink bicycle abandoned on the gravel sweep, a forgotten dog toy, a white flag on a stick that looked like the remains of a war game protruding from the side of a tree house.

And through the wide front door, with a child-sized jumper dangling from the end of the banisters and a carelessly flung shoe peeping out from behind the big grandfather clock, he could hear giggling and running footsteps.

Bedtime, he thought, his throat closing.

Oh, God, I can't do this.

But Tom was there, urging him forward, an arm

around his shoulders shepherding him through the welcoming door into the warmth and chaos of his family.

He led him down the broad hall and into the kitchen, a huge and yet homely space, the hub of the house, and there was Tom's mother, greeting him like a long-lost son, kissing his cheek, hugging him, telling him she was proud of his success. If only she knew.

But he managed to smile, to hug her back, to tell her she looked wonderful, and then Tom's father was there, shaking his hand, offering him a drink, and Tom was introducing him to Catherine, a leggy fourteen-year-old who was turning into an astonishingly beautiful young woman.

He shook her hand, trying to banish the frown that was threatening to take over his face. 'It's good to see you again, Catherine.'

'Aren't you going to say, "My, haven't you grown"?' she said, tipping her head on one side, and he felt the frown retreat, to be replaced by a grin.

'Well, I could, but since I haven't seen you for several years, I would think it's pretty obvious,' he said. 'The last time I saw you, you were probably three or four, and your brother—Andrew, is it?—was tiny.'

'He's bigger, too,' Catherine said with pithy humour, and Ben chuckled, feeling the pressure ease as she went on, 'He's around somewhere—he'll have his nose in a book. He's going to be a genius.'

The dry irony of her tone made him laugh again, and she smiled back. 'So,' she said frankly, 'what's it like to be famous?'

'Tedious,' he said without hesitation. 'I can't go shopping for clothes without people recognising me, and there's a woman in my hotel who's already—'

He broke off, unsure quite how to phrase it to this young girl, but she had it down pat.

'Cracking on to you?' she said, rolling her eyes. 'Sad. You're just a person. Dad said he was cleverer than you at uni.'

'He was,' Ben agreed with a grin, 'but I was better at the clinical stuff.'

'So why did you give up?'

For a moment, he was speechless, and the room fell totally silent, hanging on his response.

'It wasn't what I wanted to do any more,' he said finally, acknowledging at least part of the truth, if not the whys and wherefores. No doubt he'd have to explain them now, he thought, but then Catherine innocently rescued him with more of her open and ingenuous chatter.

'So you moved on? I'll buy that. It seems impossible when they ask me what I want to do—I've got to make career choices already, and I can't. I mean, it's my whole life, you know? There are so many things to do, and lots of people make career changes these days. Look at Fliss. She's a nurse, but she's been a property developer, too, and she's fantastic at it, and now she's a mum, and she's doing that for England. Fliss says change is good, it keeps your mind fit. She's cool.'

And everyone seemed to breathe again, or was Ben just imagining it?

'I'm looking forward to meeting this legend,' he said, turning to Tom and meeting that questioning and thoughtful gaze head on. 'I take it she's putting the younger ones to bed?'

'Yes. They'll be down in a minute— Ah, here you go. Darling, meet Ben. Ben, my wife, Felicity.'

The pride and love in his voice was reflected in his

eyes, and Ben felt the ache of loss. Not now, he told himself, and before he could get his armour straight again, he was enveloped in a warm, soft hug that smelt of baby oil and lavender.

You lucky, lucky man, he thought, and then, as he stepped back out of her embrace, he caught sight of Meg behind her, in the open doorway, with the sun streaming through behind her and backlighting her like an angel. She had a baby in her arms, and she was walking towards him with a wary expression that made him think she wasn't any keener to be here than he was.

'Hello again,' she said, and as she approached he was again engulfed in the same soft cloud of lavender and baby oil. Except that this time it hit him like a truck.

Since when had baby oil been so sexy? And lavender? Good grief. Old ladies smelt of lavender! And she was covered in baby powder, her hair escaping from the clip at the back and slithering down her neck, and he wanted to tunnel his fingers into it and anchor her head and kiss her senseless.

She held the baby out. 'Meet my god-daughter Charlotte,' she said with a smile for the baby, and put her in his arms. He tucked her onto his hip automatically and stared down into her serious little face. Damn, if Meg didn't stop shoving kids into his arms he was going to—

Then Charlotte gurgled, her eyes lighting up as she reached out a chubby little hand to grab his nose, and he ducked out of the way and caught her fist in his and laughed.

'Hello, toothy,' he said, and she giggled, showing her three little front teeth even more clearly. 'You're gorgeous, aren't you?' he murmured, and she beamed at him as if he was the cleverest person in the world, and he felt another twist deep inside.

'Ben, where shall I put your drink?' David Whittaker was asking, and he seized the escape route with relief.

'I'll take it. Here, Meg, have her back. She's yawning.'

He handed her back, catching a provocative glimpse of cleavage in the low V of Meg's T-shirt as the baby grabbed it. Heat slammed through him again and, almost dropping the baby in his haste, he stepped back, wrapping one hand round the proffered drink and ramming his other hand into his pocket, out of mischief. He turned back to Tom and Fliss and groped for pleasantries.

'This is a lovely place you've got here.'

Fliss laughed. 'It wasn't. It was a nightmare this time last year. We did it up.'

'We? You did it up,' Tom corrected, and turned to Ben. 'She project-managed it like a military operation. The poor builders were run ragged.'

'Ah, this property developer's hat I've been hearing about?' Ben said, latching on to a neutral topic like a drowning man with a straw. And the conversation moved on, away from children and his career and the past and all the endless questions which that topic could throw up, and into the much safer territory of the house's restoration.

They drifted out to the garden, sitting on the terrace in the warmth of the early July evening. Andrew joined them, book in hand, and chucked in the odd remark from time to time, and gradually Ben relaxed.

This wasn't so hard. They were lovely people, and if they would just accept him and leave the past alone, maybe it would be all right. And it was, for a while.

They ate simply. Salad, bread rolls warm from the oven, spicy chicken and thick juicy steaks seared on the barbeque. Under cover of the conversation Ben watched Meg. She interacted easily with the others, laughing and frowning in concentration and waving a dismissive hand to brush aside something she didn't agree with. He thought again, The camera will love her. She's a natural.

And then she turned and he caught the full force of that natural and beautiful smile, and his breath jammed in his throat.

Dear God, she was beautiful. Beautiful and warm and sexy, and he wanted her, as he hadn't wanted a woman in ages. Years. For ever, maybe. Their eyes locked, and her tongue flicked out to moisten her lips and his throat closed.

'So, this woman who's cracking on to you—as my daughter so delicately put it—is she going to be a nuisance?' Tom asked conversationally, and Ben dragged his eyes from Meg's and looked at Tom.

'Woman?'

'In the hotel.'

'Oh, her. She's a pain, but I'll cope. I'll change hotels if necessary.'

'Why don't you come here?' Fliss said, automatically swapping the baby from one breast to the other without a trace of self-consciousness. 'We've got room—tons of room. The house was designed with a staff flat which we've kept because Tom was going to have an *au pair*, and it's going begging since I rather made her job redundant. You may as well have it. It's close to the hospital, and you'll have privacy if you want it, and you can come and go when you like. You won't disturb us, because it's got its own entrance as well as the link to the house. And no women cracking on to you, I promise!'

He opened his mouth to refuse, but Fliss shook her head. 'Think about it. The offer's open. More food, any-one?'

CHAPTER THREE

BEN did think about it. Not then, but later, when he'd said his goodbyes and escaped from the gently suffocating warmth of their company and driven away into the dark and lonely night, back to the anonymous, hushed politeness of the hotel. He let himself into a room like all the hotel rooms he'd ever stayed in, perfectly well equipped and furnished, clean and fresh, with all the little bottles and potions set out in the bathroom and the tea- and coffee-making facilities on the tray by the television.

Boring as hell, utterly sterile and characterless.

Safe.

He spent his life like this now, moving from room to room, hotel to hotel, filming in odd locations and retreating each night like a hermit crab to an empty room abandoned by the previous occupant.

Not that his flat was any better. Just as stark and soulless, but that was fine. He didn't want more.

He thought of Tom and Fliss and their family, warm and chaotic and noisy and full of life and love and happiness, and he felt a well of unaccustomed emotion rising up to choke him.

'Stupid,' he muttered. 'I don't need all that.'

And then there was a knock at the door. 'Ben?'

Ah, no. Not her. He needed her even less.

'Ben? I know you're in there. I've got something for you.'

I'll bet, he thought, a shudder running through him.

He said nothing, and after a few minutes she went away. He started to relax, but too soon. His phone rang—not his mobile, which he would have answered, but the one by the bed. He ignored it. Minutes later there was another knock at the door.

'Room service,' a male voice said.

'I didn't order anything. I don't want it,' he said, and there was a murmured conversation outside the door, and then fading footsteps, hushed by the carpet.

He held his breath. She was still there, he'd stake his life on it. Suddenly tired of it, tired of the fame, the lack of privacy, the empty futility of his life, he catapulted off the bed and yanked open the door.

'I'm not interested. Please, go away and leave me alone. I'm tired. I don't need this.'

'It's just a little bottle of something,' she coaxed, her lashes fluttering. He looked down at her, sad and lonely and desperate, and thought of Meg.

Meg, who was warm and vibrant and funny, not afraid to speak her mind. Meg, who he was going to be shadowing for the next week, all day, every day.

And, if his hormones had a say in it, every minute of the night as well.

But not tonight, unfortunately, and his hormones were not so desperate that they'd take this woman up on her offer under any circumstances.

'I'm sorry,' he said, hanging on to his manners with difficulty. 'I've had a long day, I've got a long week ahead. Please—leave me alone.'

And he shut the door, locked it firmly and went to bed.

Meg thought she'd have trouble sleeping, but she didn't. Not at all. In fact, she slept all night, wrapped in a web of dreams all of which seemed to feature yours truly in glorious Technicolor.

Glorious being the operative word.

It was almost a relief when she woke to her alarm at five, because she could pull on her running shorts and vest, with its front pocket for her phone and keys, and head out onto the sleeping streets, pounding the pavements until she reached the little park that ran alongside the road and could shift across onto the dew-soaked grass under the trees.

She loved this time of day, before the world really got moving and started to crowd in on her. Not that she minded the people. She loved people. It was just that sometimes she needed to be alone, and five o'clock in the morning was definitely one of those times.

She headed back, sweat trickling down her spine and between her breasts, soaking into the vest top and the waistband of her shorts as she slowed her pace and walked back down the last little street to her flat.

By the time she'd reached the top floor and stripped off, it was five twenty-three, and by the time she'd stepped out of the cool, refreshing shower, with her hair streaming and her skin alive from the scrubbing, it was five thirty-one.

And Ben was going to be at the hospital at six, complete with make-up crew.

That was a problem. Meg didn't do make-up, ever, under any circumstances. She hated the feel of it on her skin, and her lashes were long enough to brush the lenses of her sunnies, so what was the point of mascara? And if she put eyeshadow on, it would only be a very natural colour, and since she had deep sockets and wide eyes, that, too, seemed pointless. And as for lipstick, the nearest she ever got was a flick of lipgloss.

Besides, she was going to work, not to play.

She dried her hair, grateful to it for lying smooth and flat for once and not drying into a kink, and then scraped it back anyway and twisted it up on the back of her head and secured it with a clip. Thank heavens for the decent cut and the miracle of conditioner, she thought, and also for the glow of health her holiday in the sun had given her skin.

And then she stopped preening and dallying in front of the mirror, dragged on the—beautifully pressed for once!—tunic top and trousers of her uniform and ran downstairs to her car. She pulled into the hospital car park at a minute to six, found a slot by a miracle and screeched into the department at three minutes past.

'Thought you'd bottled out,' a low voice murmured behind her, and she jumped and spun round, her heart skittering. She could feel her eyes widening, feel her nostrils flaring to draw in the scent of soap on freshly washed skin, the faint citrus tang of shampoo, and something else, something masculine and dangerous and very, very exciting.

Ben's eyes tracked over her, and before she could speak or move or do anything, he lifted a hand and trailed a warm, slightly rough fingertip over her skin— across her cheek, over her nose, down her jaw, down, to the hollow of her throat where her pulse beat frantically under his touch.

'Been running?' he murmured, and she sucked in a breath and stepped back.

'I run every morning,' she said, almost truthfully. Especially, she could have added, when I've had a man like you in my dreams all night and my hormones need exorcising, like a ghost, as opposed to exercising, like they were all night!

'That explains the healthy glow. Let's go and talk to Jude.'

'Jude?'

'Make-up.'

She opened her mouth to argue with him, but he'd gone, turned on his heel and vanished through the double doors and down the corridor towards Matt's commandeered office, clearly anticipating that she would follow. Which, of course, she did, but it would have been nice to be asked, she thought crossly.

By the time she caught up with him he was lolling in the doorway, chatting to a woman with pink hair and black lipstick.

'Ah, Jude, this is Meg.'

Meg stared at the woman with a sinking heart. There was no way she'd convince someone who could do that to herself that the bare, unadorned look was how she'd like to be.

Or so she thought. Jude, however, was obviously deeper than the tattoos that covered every visible inch of her body.

She sat Meg down, ran a finger over her skin—just like Ben, only without provoking the heart attack—and sat back with a gusty sigh. 'Flawless,' she said, and shut her make-up box. 'I don't want to do anything to her, other than maybe a flick of dust to take the shine off if it gets too hot. Let's see how she is on camera. If you aren't using lights, I don't see a problem.'

Ben nodded. 'Good. I'm glad we agree.'

Pete Harrison, the producer, stuck his head round the door and winked at Meg. 'Our star,' he said, coming in and taking her hand, squeezing it rather too earnestly as he stared into her eyes. 'Good to see you're on time. Looking forward to it?'

Meg snorted and extracted her hand from his before he crushed it. 'Not exactly.'

'You should. You'll be great.'

Meg wished she had his confidence. Once that camera started rolling, and her mouth opened—well, it just didn't bear thinking about. But clearly Pete wasn't worried in the least. Probably because he didn't realise just how worried he ought to be. Well, time would sort that one out!

His eyes flicked to Jude. 'When you've done her make-up, give me a shout.'

'It's done—she doesn't need any,' Jude said.

He nodded. 'The flawless skin of extreme youth,' he sighed, and Meg laughed.

'Hardly. I'm twenty-six.'

'That's extreme youth compared to Pete,' Ben said, and earned himself a black look from the producer.

He sucked in his stomach and turned back to Meg. 'OK, Meg, let's roll. I think the easiest thing to do is follow you, and let you do whatever you would normally do.'

'What about permission from the patients?' she asked, belatedly worrying about that and wondering if it might give her an out. 'How do you get consent to use the footage?'

'We deal with that individually,' he explained. 'We've put up a sign saying we're filming in the department to warn people, and Rae, our researcher, will get consents from everyone we film. If they're unconscious, we ask them or their relatives later. But we aren't here to offend, and we can do a lot with blurring and narration so the identities of the patients are protected. I'm thinking here of RTAs, multiple trauma, anything gory. We can always edit out the worst of the blood. What we don't want is you sitting in a room doing endless ankle supports and splinters, and Matt and Tom are fine with that. As much action as possible is the order of the day.'

Thank God, Meg thought, because there was no way she wanted to sit and do ankles all day either. Although if they wanted her holding anyone's head while they were sick, they could whistle, because she was lousy at it!

Pete glanced at his watch. 'Right. We've got a few minutes before you're due to start, so I'd like to get a bit on camera and check the make-up really is OK. We need to get you miked up as well.'

Which involved having a small microphone clipped to her lapel and a small but surprisingly heavy battery pack strapped to her back under her tunic. Great for the figure, she thought. I've got enough under there without any extra bumps!

But strapped on it was, and then Ben was asking her questions, and they were testing sound levels and lighting levels and running it back so they could see, and Meg thought, Lord, it really is happening. I'm going to be on this stupid programme!

'Right. It's five to seven, so we need to film you arriving for work. Can you get your car and drive in and park it?'

'What—and lose my parking space? You must be crazy! Anyway, I don't want my car identified if possible. I don't want to become a target for weirdos.'

'Why don't we film her walking in through the doors?' Ben suggested, so they went to the entrance and set up the shot, but someone got in the way and so she had to go out again, and then again, and of course she forgot that she had the radio mike on, so by the time she came through the doors for the third time they were chuckling.

'"Oh, pooh"?' Steve, the camera and sound man, said with a teasing look, and she blushed furiously and smacked her forehead with her palm. She hadn't even had to talk and she'd said the wrong thing already!

'I'm sorry! I'll do it again,' she wailed, but they told her not to worry.

'They' being Pete, Steve—an outrageous flirt who had put Meg instantly at her ease with his silly banter— and Rae the researcher, tiny and looking young enough to be at school.

'We can work round that footage,' Steve said, and Pete nodded.

'Right. Better get inside and see what's going on, and if you could moderate the language it'll save a lot of those bleeps,' Pete teased. 'What we need now,' he went on, 'is something good and dramatic to kick off with.' And right on queue, they heard the sirens.

'Traumatic amputation coming in following an accident in a glasshouse—want to do this one, Meg?' Angie asked, appearing at her elbow.

Pete's eyes lit up, and Meg chuckled.

'You must have some amazing influence,' she said with a rueful grin, and, donning gloves and a disposable apron, she headed for the doors.

It was a good job Ben was a doctor and Steve didn't seem to be fazed by the sight of blood, because when the ambulance doors opened there was plenty of it to see.

Meg, forgetting all about them, moved straight in and started asking questions, listening to the report from the paramedics, a bag of saline held aloft as they pulled the trolley out of the ambulance, locked its legs down and hurried through to Resus. Kenna was on the other side, holding a pressure pad on the elevated stump to try and minimise blood loss, while Mike filled Meg in.

'Andy Johnson, farmer, aged thirty-six, working in a glasshouse when part of the roof fell in and sliced his hand off. He's had morphine and we've started him on fluids, but BP's stable at 130 over 70. No other visible injuries and the bleeding's under control.'

'Thanks. I think we know him, actually.' Meg bent over him, making eye contact and smiling to reassure him, the film team forgotten. 'Hi again, Andy, I'm Meg. We met last time you were in. I'm going to be staying with you while you're in the accident and emergency department, so anything you want to know, feel free to ask me. How are you feeling? How's the pain?'

'OK now, wearing off thanks to these guys. Bloody cross with myself, though,' Andy growled weakly from the trolley. 'I can't believe it. I knew the glass was loose, but I never dreamt...' He shook his head in disgust. 'It's a nightmare—how the hell am I going to cope with one hand? I thought losing the finger was bad enough.'

'Let's cross one bridge at a time,' Meg said soothingly, and glanced up at Mike, the paramedic who'd given her the report. 'Do we have the hand?'

'Yes—I've got it here,' Kenna said. 'It's in pretty good condition, considering the dog retrieved it.'

Meg's heart sank. 'The dog?'

'Ran into the kitchen—that's how his wife found out,' she was told as Kenna handed her the plastic bag with the hand in it packed in saline swabs. 'They're following—Mrs Johnson and two children. They'll be here shortly.'

'Andy? Andy!'

'That's Jill,' Andy said, lifting his head, but Meg pushed him gently back.

'Don't worry about her. Someone will look after her and fill her in. She can come and see you in a minute. Sophie, could you do that, please? You just lie there and relax and let us do our job. Right, let's shift him across on my count, please—one, two, three.'

They slid Andy across onto the bed, taking care to support his damaged arm and the pillow it was elevated on. Meg clipped the bag of saline onto the drip stand and took over the pressure from Kenna while Angie hooked him up to the monitor. He sagged back against the pillows, then his eyes flicked past Meg and he frowned in concentration. 'Do I know you? Aren't you on the telly?' he said, and out of the corner of her eye Meg saw Ben move forward.

Heavens. She'd forgotten about him.

'Ben Maguire,' he said. 'We're filming in the department.'

Andy gave a grim little laugh. 'So do I get to be on the telly? Blimey. You'd better get the missus on too, or my life won't be worth living.'

'I'm sure that would be fine,' Ben said, and Meg wondered if she was hearing things or if his voice was unusually curt. Yes, she thought as he carried on, giving the researcher her instructions. Definitely curt. 'Rae, could you talk to them when someone's filled them in on his condition? Background would be good.'

'Sure,' Rae agreed, and Meg shot him a sideways look.

Yup. He was as tense as hell, his hands rammed in his pockets, far from the casual, relaxed presenter of his earlier programmes. So why—?

'Ben Maguire, eh? How about that?' Andy murmured, his voice slurring a little with the pain relief. 'I'd shake hands, mate, but it's in a plastic bag at the moment.'

Ben laughed shortly and patted his shoulder. 'I'll consider us formally introduced, under the circumstances. You just lie there and let them fix you up.'

Tom had come in by now, and was busy checking the condition of the stump, issuing instructions for the pressure pad, his eye running over the monitor and assessing Andy's vital signs. Although the bleeding seemed under control now, Andy was pale and clammy, and he'd obviously lost a considerable amount before they'd got to him.

'Right, let's have some bloods—is that saline or Ringer's lactate running in?'

'Saline. I've taken bloods,' Meg said, reeling off the list, and Tom nodded.

'Right, better switch to Ringer's now. We'll go for two units to start with. Hopefully we won't need blood products. What about the hand? Anyone checked the condition yet?'

'I have—it's looking good,' Angie said. 'It's packed in saline swabs and I've put the bag in cool water and notified the hand surgeon. He'll be down any minute.'

'Good. Well, Andy, it's a nice clean cut straight through the radius and ulna—textbook amputation. If you had to do it, you made a good job of it,' Tom said with a reassuring smile. 'I should say the chances of reattaching it are good.'

Andy closed his eyes and swallowed. 'Thank God for that. You couldn't save the finger, but I can manage without that. The hand might be a whole different ball game. I couldn't see my wife, could I?' he asked, the

momentary distraction of Ben's presence obviously
wearing off and leaving him acutely aware of the grav-
ity of the situation.

'Sure. I'll go and talk to her, shall I?' Meg asked
Tom, and he nodded.

She expected Ben and Steve to stay there and carry
on filming, but to her surprise they followed her out
into the corridor, where she found Mrs Johnson standing
staring at the resus door, bracketed by two young children—seven and nine or thereabouts, Meg thought, and
certainly old enough for the events to have registered
with them. They looked worried and overawed.

Until they saw Ben. Then the elder one straightened
up, his eyes widening. 'Mum? Look who it is!'

'Mrs Johnson?' Meg said, and the woman's eyes
flicked from her to Ben and back, focusing on what
mattered.

'Meg?'

'Hello, Jill. Are you OK?'

'Not really. Oh, thank God it's you. How is he?
How's Andy?'

'OK. He'll need surgery, but he's stable and the
hand's looking good. The hand surgeon will come down
in a minute and see him and decide if it's possible to
reattach it, if the dog hasn't done it too much damage.'

'Oh, he won't have done. He's a spaniel—very soft
mouth—and he brought it straight to me in the kitchen.
We were having breakfast, and the next thing was the
dog ran in and the kids screamed. I thought it was something disgusting at first, but then I realised what it was,
and I knew straight away it was Andy's, because of the
finger. If Rufus hadn't brought it—well, I hate to think
what would have happened. I might have gone out with
the kids and left Andy there...' She broke off, tortured

by the horrors of what might have been, and Meg put an arm around her and hugged her.

'But you didn't,' she said, 'and he's here, and he's going to be fine. Come on, come and see him.'

'Can we come?' the boys asked, and she nodded and ushered them all towards Resus, the children gathered into her other arm.

'Come on, all of you come in and see him for a minute. He's asking for you.'

'Will the kids be all right in there?' Jill asked anxiously.

'They'll be fine,' Meg assured her. 'There's all sorts of equipment, but we're just keeping an eye on him, it's nothing to worry about.'

'Is there lots of blood?' the little one asked, his eyes wide and hopeful.

'No, not really. We've cleaned it up.'

'Oh,' he said, crestfallen, and Meg grinned.

'Bloodthirsty little monster,' his mother said affectionately, and then looked at Ben. 'Are you really Ben Maguire?'

He nodded, his mouth tilting into something that was almost a smile. 'For my sins. We're filming in the department. Is it all right to follow you?'

'Wow, Mum, we'll be on the telly!' the elder one said, and his brother perked up again and looked suitably impressed.

Meg was glad. It would take their minds off their father, and that could only be a good thing at the moment.

Their visit was only brief, but it was enough to reassure them that he was alive and staying that way, and then she ushered them to the relatives' room and left them with Sophie in charge of drinks and biscuits.

A quarter of an hour later Andy was off to Theatre, the hand having been declared viable. Meg had time to register that the whole scene had been recorded, warts and all, and she had blood smeared on her cheek and her uniform was trashed and all her careful pressing had been in vain.

She turned to the camera, looking full into it for the first time.

'That bloodthirsty enough for you?' she said cheekily, and Pete chuckled.

'I think that'll satisfy even the most ghoulish of our viewers. Can we talk it through?' he asked, but she shook her head.

'Give me five? I need to change into fresh clothes before the next case descends on us, and we'll catch up then.'

'Any chance of a coffee?' Steve said hopefully, and Meg pointed them in the direction of the staffroom.

'Help yourselves. I'll be with you in a tick,' she said, and hurried off.

'Meg?'

She stopped and turned, to find Ben following her. His hand reached up towards her breast, and her heart lurched, but then it settled as he unclipped the mike from her lapel and dropped it down the neck of her tunic.

Idiot! What on earth did she think he'd been about to do?

She undid the belt, slid off the battery pack and handed it to him wordlessly, then turned and retreated to the relative safety of the changing room.

She didn't know what the hell was eating him, but he'd been almost silent throughout Andy's treatment. If he wasn't going to talk, to ask her anything or comment, the programme was going to be vastly different to all the others.

She shrugged. It was hardly her problem, and, anyway, the last thing she needed when she was working was someone asking her stupid questions. She ought to be relieved.

So why was she worrying about Ben instead?

One down, however many to go, Ben thought, and turned and followed the others into the staffroom.

'Well, that went fine,' Pete said, rubbing his hands together and grinning. 'How obliging of that man to cut his hand off for us—and they know him, too, so lots of touchy-feely. Excellent. Very dramatic—brilliant start, don't you think, Ben?'

Ben didn't. Ben thought Pete was sick, but that was nothing new. He shot him a withering look, then turned to Rae. 'Did you talk to his wife?'

She nodded. 'Yes, she's fine with it, and the kids think it's great. I've got the consents. Here, have a coffee.'

'Cheers.'

He took it from her, taking a gulp and burning his tongue. Damn. He needed to concentrate, not think about Meg and what it had been like to watch her hands working deftly on their patient.

No. *Her* patient. Not *theirs*. It was nothing to do with him. He didn't work here, and it was just as well, because his heart had been racing and his legs had turned to jelly.

Not because of Andy Johnson, not because of the blood or the sight of his wound or because of watching Meg, but the noises, so familiar, so evocative, so—

The coffee slopped, burning his hand and bringing him slamming back to the present with a jolt.

'Damn,' he muttered, and ran his hand under cold water.

'You OK?' Rae asked, her eyes curious, as well they might be. This was most unlike him. Normally he was utterly laid-back, laughing and joking with the others between shots, totally easygoing.

Not now. Not here, in this damned hospital, torn between dread and a totally unprecedented lust for a woman he knew nothing about, whose life he was about to become privy to in intimate and microscopic detail.

Every last nuance of her days would become his, the highs, the lows, the in-betweens—all of it, on and off duty—because that was how the programme worked.

And beyond even the bounds of duty, he wanted the rest, the bits no one would ever see, the utterly private and off-limits moments his body was screaming for.

Crazy.

'I'm fine,' he muttered, and then she came in, her smile turning on the sun, driving out the shadows and riveting his attention on her with the brush of her startling eyes.

'Anybody made me one?'

He would have done it if he'd been able to move, but his muscles didn't seem to belong to him. And anyway Rae had done it, Rae, calm and unflappable and brilliantly organised, keeping them all in order and ticking all the boxes, so all he had to do was stand and look at Meg, draped in the curiously sexy pale blue theatre scrubs that she'd changed into.

Scrubs? Sexy? Sheesh, he was in trouble.

He gulped the coffee, cooler now so it didn't precipitate a crisis, and watched her in amazement.

How could she turn something so sexless, so shapeless, into something so incredibly alluring? It didn't seem possible.

She sloshed cold water into her cup, drained it and turned to him. 'Right, I'd better have my mike back on and then we need to get back to work.'

'We were going to talk through that last case,' Pete reminded her, but she shook her head.

'Not now. We're too busy—the waiting time's up to three hours. Mondays are always chaos, with all the little things people have been sitting on over the weekend while they've been too busy. It'll settle down, though. If there's a gap later we can do it then.'

'And if there isn't?'

She shrugged. 'We'll do it after I've finished.'

'But we need more information—'

'Then you'll have to wait. I thought the idea was that you shadowed me. So shadow. I don't stand still, I can't. If you want to shadow something easy, go find a tree.'

Ben felt his mouth twitch, but Meg was right there in front of him, holding out her hand palm up. He passed her the mike and tried not to watch as she threaded it up through the top of the scrubs and clipped it on the open V. Then she slipped the belt round her waist and tightened it to hold the battery pack in place, and he turned it on again.

'How's that?' she asked, looking at Steve, and he nodded.

'Fine, got you.'

'Right, let's go,' she said, and without ado she went out, leaving them all to follow.

'Grumpy mare,' Pete muttered, and Ben gave him another killing look.

'She's right—hospitals are busy places, and she doesn't have time for us. She can't dangle about while you cross all your T's and dot your I's.'

'So ask the relevant bloody questions instead of standing there with your hands in your pockets,' Pete growled, and Ben felt a surge of irrational anger, because he knew his producer was right.

'I was giving her space until she was used to us,' he retorted, keeping his temper with difficulty. There was a grain of truth in his reply, but no more than a grain. The rest of it was to do with keeping a low profile and keeping his emotions under control.

And that didn't seem to be working at all.

CHAPTER FOUR

IN CONTRAST to that morning, the rest of the day went dead. Not that they weren't busy, because they were, but it was a constant stream of the sort of things she sensed Pete didn't like.

Not cutting edge enough, not enough blood and guts.

Ben, however, started getting involved and asking more questions, although Meg could still feel the tension coming off him in waves. She wondered if he was always like this and the editing just took care of the growly bits, or if it was a simple personality clash with her—perhaps because she'd told him he didn't need to get to know her that well?

Well, tough. She didn't want to be doing the programme either, and she was stuck with it, so he could just darned well cope. At least he was being paid to do it. She was just doing her job, and having him and the rest of the crew hanging around was most definitely *not* a perk!

A child came in with something stuffed in his ear and, with Ben to distract him and keep him occupied on his mother's knee, Meg was able to use suction to get the foreign body out.

'There,' she said, showing him the little bead, and his mother sighed with relief and fluttered her eyelashes at Ben.

His answering smile was warm—too warm—and Meg felt an uncharacteristic flash of jealousy and had to look away before the camera caught her glaring at

him. Why should she feel like that? So he was very
decorative and charming—well, he could be, some of
the time. And intriguing for the rest of it.

But—could she really be jealous? Because he'd
smiled at the boy's mother and made her laugh?

Ridiculous.

She gave the bead back to the mother and sent them
off, then pulled a splinter out from under a nail, put a
support on an ankle declared by Nick Baker to be just
a nasty sprain and gave the appropriate advice—MICE,
short for mobilisation, ice, compression and elevation—
and a set of crutches, gave a child an emetic to make
her sick after she'd possibly taken some of her mother's
herbal weight-loss pills and then discovered the pills
when they fell out of the child's pocket as the little one
was busy retching over yet another set of scrubs…

Retching, while Meg held on to her stomach contents
with difficulty and wondered why she'd been lumbered
with this one.

But Ben was asking her stupid questions and Steve
dutifully recorded her answers and Pete twitched and
hovered in the background, no doubt wishing the sky
would fall in and cause a major incident to give the
programme some zip.

No such luck. She might have been busy enough,
then, to put Ben out of her mind, but as it was he was
right there, right under her nose with his sexy grin and
his rumpled hair and the stubble that darkened his jaw
as the day wore on.

Then as she emerged from the cubicle with the evidence of the emetic still splattered over her front, Tom
caught up with them.

'So, how's it been?'

'Dull,' she said, getting in before Pete could.

Ben shrugged. 'It's just swings and roundabouts. That's how it is. It's fine.'

Tom grinned. 'Don't get too comfortable. It'll pick up for sure just before I knock off. Meg, while I think about it, they need some more sponsor forms on the front desk. Ben, are you joining Meg on Saturday for this lunatic plunge to doom?'

'Lunatic plunge?' Ben said, and her heart crashed into her throat.

'Did you have to remind me?' she groaned.

'What lunatic plunge?' Ben said again, his face puzzled.

'A charity abseil,' Tom told him, and Meg gave another groan.

Damn. It had totally escaped her mind because of Ben and this filming nonsense, and now she felt sick all over again.

'I'd forgotten,' she mumbled. 'Oh, rats.'

But Tom was telling Ben all about it. 'They go off the top of the surgical block—that great tall thing. It's a massive event—draws a huge crowd and raises a fortune every year.'

'Cheers, Tom,' she said drily—very drily. Her throat had closed and her tongue was stuck to the roof of her mouth with fear. 'And can we have less of the great tall thing stuff? I'd totally forgotten,' she said again, wondering how she could possibly have let something that terrified her so much completely slip her mind.

'And you're doing this?' Ben asked, and she nodded.

'For my sins. And for the new 3-D scanner. We do it every year for some damn piece of equipment or other, and every year without fail I seem to get sucked in.'

'I'll sponsor you,' he said, and she turned to him, laughing in disbelief.

'Like hell you'll sponsor me,' she said. 'Don't think you're getting away with it that lightly. You're shadowing me, Maguire—and that means you're doing it with me, every last blasted inch of it. It's the least you can do.'

He backed up, his arms folded defensively across his chest, his head shaking firmly from side to side.

'Oh, no.'

'Oh, yes. Sorry, it's not negotiable. I'll get you a sponsor form.'

'I don't do stunts.'

'It's not a stunt,' she said patiently. 'It's a charity fund-raiser. And, believe me, you're doing it. You're shadowing me, and if I have to, then you have to. End of story. Trust me, nobody wants to do it less than I do.'

And she turned on her heel, snatched the next set of notes and headed for the waiting room.

Ben shook his head and stared after her, then turned to Pete, ready to share a joke about stroppy women, to find his producer grinning cheerfully.

'Great. Excellent. Abseiling for charity—couldn't be better.'

'Who for?' Ben muttered. 'Hell's teeth, Pete.'

'It's nothing. Falling off a log.'

Or a high building. Very high. Extremely high. 'So you do it if it's so damned easy,' he suggested.

'Oh, no.' Pete laughed, holding up his hands. 'I'm a nobody.'

'Glad you realise it.'

'But you, on the other hand, are not, and as part of the programme—well, it's like manna from heaven.'

'No.'

'You don't have a choice,' Pete reminded him, and he got the overwhelming urge to deck him. Again.

'You'll wear that trump card out if you aren't careful,' he growled, curling his fists in his pockets and hanging on for dear life.

Pete looked at him, his eyes narrowing, then he grinned that slow barracuda grin. 'You're scared!' he said with relish. 'You great big girl's blouse!'

Ben shot him a look and stalked off to find Meg. She was already ensconced in a cubicle, and Rae was there, checking details and charming the patient into agreeing to the filming.

Damn. Why couldn't they all refuse, and he could go home?

'I've got your sponsor form,' Meg told him in a rare quiet moment. 'Here.'

He looked down at it in her outstretched hand, and shook his head.

'No. You get me your half-dozen or so sponsors, and I'll pay up what they would have given, but I'm not doing it.'

She ran her eyes over his face, over the determined eyes and the mutinous set of his mouth, and laughed.

'We'll see,' she said, and he just raised a brow, but it didn't impress her. Besides, she had an idea, and once she'd finally escaped from Pete and his endless urge to go over the day's footage, she put her plan into action.

Hanging up after the last phone call, she smiled smugly.

'Get out of that, Maguire,' she said to the empty room. Curling up in her favourite chair with a cup of tea and the TV remote, she settled down for an evening of channel-hopping.

Nothing. Even with cable, there was nothing.

She eyed the pile of video tapes on the floor. Tapes of Ben's programmes, courtesy of her mother, a passionate fan forced to record them because they clashed with something her father would rather watch.

And she hadn't seen them all.

She put the first one in and watched it, fluctuating between laughter and tears and nail-biting tension, and wondering what had happened to the easygoing, sensitive and fun-loving person in the video to change him into the crotchety, awkward and uptight man she'd been dealing with all day.

Was it her? Or the situation?

The situation, she decided, because during the war correspondent one she'd just watched, when they got a bit close to the medical bits after one of the soldiers had been badly injured and airlifted out, he grew tense and withdrawn.

Once more she wondered why Ben had given up medicine. Maybe the other tapes would hold the clue, she thought, and reached for the next.

The smell hit Ben the moment he opened the door.

Stunned, he shut it behind him, staring round, searching for the source, and then he found it.

Lilies, a huge vase of them—white lilies, their scent cloying in the closed room. Suffocating him. Of all the things—

There was a tap on the door. 'Ben? Did you like the flowers?'

He hardly heard her. Hardly heard anything over the roaring in his ears and the pounding of his heart.

His mouth watered suddenly, and he swallowed hard, forcing down the nausea.

Open the window. That's the thing. Open the window.

But it wasn't enough. The scent was choking him, dredging up a memory he'd buried so deep he'd thought it could never surface.

Ignoring her, ignoring the lilies, he picked up his mobile and went into the bathroom, shutting the door firmly. Scanning through the index for Tom's home number, he pressed the call button with shaking fingers and got Fliss after two rings.

'You offered me a room,' he said without preamble. 'Is the offer still open?'

'Ben! Sure, of course. Do you want to come now? Is she giving you trouble?'

He gave a strangled laugh. 'You could say that. Do you mind?'

'I'd be delighted,' she said. 'I'll make the bed now. Come on over.'

'I can make the bed. Give me five minutes.'

He slid the phone back into his pocket, took a deep breath and went back into the bedroom, wash bag in hand. It took seconds to throw his clothes into his case, then he wrenched open the door and went out, desperate for air. The woman was in the hall, a smile hovering on her lips, but she took one look at his face and her smile vanished.

'Ben?' she said tentatively, but he didn't even look at her.

'There are laws about stalking people,' he grated. Brushing her aside, he strode down the corridor, took the stairs down two at a time, because it was quicker than waiting for the lift, and accosted the receptionist.

'I'd like to check out,' he said curtly, slapping his key card down on the desk. 'Pete Harrison will settle the bill. And some flowers were delivered to my room in error. Dispose of them, please.'

'Ben? Please, let me explain…'

'There's nothing to explain. I don't know you. Leave me alone.'

The manager emerged then from the inner office and ran after him with a worried look on his face.

'Sir! Mr Maguire!' he called, but Ben just jerked a thumb at the woman and said, 'Don't let her follow me.'

He arrived at the Red House in a flurry of gravel, and Fliss opened the door, kissed his cheek and took him up to the flat.

'Make yourself at home. I've put tea and coffee and milk in the kitchen, but I've only just turned the fridge on so it won't be cold for a while. Have you eaten? Tom's not back yet, so I can feed you, too, if you like?'

He opened his mouth to tell her not to worry and his stomach rumbled loudly.

'I'll take that as a yes,' she said with a grin, then added gently, 'I'm glad you've come. Tom's going to be so pleased. He's really missed you.' And leaving him to it, she ran down the back stairs and disappeared.

He stood there for a moment, ridiculously touched by the genuine warmth of her welcome, then he turned and studied his surroundings.

The flat was small and simple—a double bedroom, a little sitting room with a small kitchen area, and a bathroom—but it was so homely, so welcoming. There were flowers on the window-sill, but garden flowers, pretty and uncomplicated, sweet peas and roses and tall spikes of something white he didn't recognize. But they'd been

put there for him, arranged with a pure simplicity that
brought a lump to his throat.

Swallowing hard, he unpacked, made himself a cup
of tea and was settling down to drink it when a boy
with Tom's eyes appeared in the doorway.

'Are you Ben?' he asked, and Ben nodded warily.

'I'm Michael. Abby's in the bath,' he added inconsequentially, and Ben realised he must be one of the
twins that he hadn't met yesterday. Michael made himself at home on the other end of the sofa, pyjama-clad
legs crossed, regarding him thoughtfully.

'You any good at reading stories?' he asked, and Ben
gave a chuckle that sounded rusty even to his ears.

'I don't know. Probably not.'

'Thought not. Dad's useless, so's Mum. Fliss is much
better. Meg's good, too. She reads much more than
Fliss. Fliss says she's a sucker, but I like her. Can I
watch the telly?'

'Michael?'

'Is that your father calling you?' Ben asked a little
desperately, and Michael ran to the top of the stairs.

'I'm here. I'm watching telly with Ben.'

Stretching the truth a little, Ben thought, but then
Tom appeared in the doorway and threw him a grin
when he saw the blank, dark screen.

'Sorry about the invasion. Coming to join us for a
pre-dinner drink?' he asked, and Ben, suddenly finding
the thought of being alone unpalatable, nodded.

'Don't mind if I do,' he said, and followed Tom
downstairs. There he met Abby, Michael's twin sister,
sitting in the dog's bed with the dog draped patiently
over her lap, the fur on its head and neck arranged into
little palm trees with rubber bands. Abby was putting

in another band, so deeply involved with torturing the dog that she didn't even notice his arrival.

Ben suppressed a smile and took the glass of wine Tom pressed into his hand.

'Not going anywhere tonight, are you?'

Ben shook his head. 'No.'

'No drunken orgies? I thought all you TV types lived on the wild side.'

He raised an eyebrow. 'I'm getting a bit old for that now, Tom—as well you know,' he pointed out with a smile.

'Hmm. You should be married with kids by now.'

He schooled his expression. 'What—so you don't have to suffer alone?' he joked, and Tom laughed.

'Suffer? I love them all to bits.'

'Daddy, look at Amber!'

He glanced down and groaned.

'What are you doing in there? You've just had a bath.'

'So's Amber. Look at her hair, Daddy!'

So he looked, bending over to talk to the poor dog who seemed to be loving every minute of it, and Ben crossed to the window and stood staring out down the garden, his fingers anchored on the edge of the stone sink, the knuckles white.

He heard Fliss come into the room and call the children, then the creak of a sofa and the murmur of her voice reading aloud. It was unbearably cosy, and he was wondering if he could cope with it when Tom spoke.

'What happened with Jane?'

The quiet voice right behind him made him stiffen.

'Does it matter?'

'I don't know. I just know that you dropped out of

our lives very suddenly, and she wouldn't talk about it. Did you have an affair?'

Ben shook his head. 'No. God, no.'

'But she wanted to.'

For a moment he hesitated, then he sighed and dropped his head forwards in defeat. 'Yes, she wanted to. I wouldn't play ball.'

'That would have annoyed her. She liked to have her own way.'

Ben laughed softly. 'Yes. In the end she set me up— phoned and invited me round when she knew you would be out. Let's just say she was hardly dressed for entertaining.'

'Ah.'

'Indeed. So I thought it was best to get out of the way.'

'And you couldn't tell me because you didn't want to drop her in it.'

'No. I didn't want to destroy what little chance of happiness I felt you had with her. You had the kids, Tom. It wasn't fair.'

He felt his friend's hand close over his shoulder and squeeze. 'Thank you for trying. It was a wasted gesture, though. It must have been shortly afterwards that she got pregnant with the twins. It just put the kybosh on what little chance we had, but we're all right now.'

His hand fell away, and Ben turned, scanning the room, but they were alone, the children and Fliss having gone out without him noticing.

'So when did you meet Fliss?'

'Last year, when I came to the hospital. Jane and I were divorced, we'd moved here to make a new life close to my parents, and, lo and behold, there she was— the best thing that's ever happened to me.'

'You talking about me again?' Fliss said, coming back into the room without the children, and Ben watched Tom's face light up with love.

His throat closed and he turned away, staring out into the garden again and wondering if there was anything sufficiently horrendous that he could do to Pete for putting him through this.

Then Fliss's arm slipped through his and she smiled up at him. 'How about rainbow trout and boiled new potatoes and a green salad?' she suggested, and he gave her a smile he knew was crooked, but it was the best he could do.

'Sounds good. Thanks.'

She tugged him gently out of the way and busied herself at the sink, refusing his offer of help, so he went and sat down at the table and listened to Tom going through Andrew's chemistry homework.

'Sorry, it's revoltingly domestic,' Fliss said, not looking in the least apologetic, and he dredged up another smile.

'It's really kind of you to have me here, so please don't apologise,' he said, because after all it was hardly their fault that it was so damned hard to sit there surrounded by all that wedded bliss.

Although what he'd done to deserve having baby Charlotte dumped on his lap a moment later, he couldn't imagine. Catherine had brought her down because she was crying, and Fliss's hands were full, so he ended up with her, grizzly and unhappy and trying to wriggle out of his arms.

'She needs supper. Be a darling and shovel this into her,' Fliss said, and plonked a bowl of goo down in front of him.

He put them together more or less successfully, doing

fine until Charlotte decided she'd had enough and spat out the last mouthful onto her hands and grabbed his shirt to haul herself to her feet.

'Oh, you little horror!' Fliss exclaimed, grabbing a handful of kitchen roll.

Within moments he and Charlotte were cleaned up and she was whisked away to bed by her father, Andrew trailing behind and leaving him alone in the kitchen with Fliss.

Fliss topped up his glass and sat down opposite him, ripping up salad leaves and mixing oil and balsamic vinegar in a jug. 'So tell me, how are you getting on with Meg?' she asked as she worked.

He shrugged. 'OK. I don't think she's really enjoying it.'

Fliss eyed him thoughtfully. 'Funny, she said the same about you.'

He gave a short, humourless laugh. 'Perceptive of her.'

'Is it to do with why you gave up medicine?'

He looked away, dropping his eyes to his glass, giving the simple Pinot Grigio very much more attention than it deserved.

'I had reasons. They still exist,' was all he said, and Fliss let it drop and didn't mention it again over the course of the evening.

He was under no illusions about her being satisfied with his reply, but she was a sensitive and thoughtful woman, and she at least knew when to back off.

Unlike Meg.

She started on him again the following morning.

A family were brought in following an RTA—a stupid, low-speed crash in town traffic during the school run—that shouldn't by rights have hurt any of them, but the toddler hadn't been restrained, and he was furious.

And it didn't help that Meg was sympathising with the frantic mother.

'He just wouldn't stay in his seat! He won't—he's learned how to undo the straps, and he's just so naughty, and now he's hurt…'

She broke off, sobbing, and Meg hugged her briefly.

'It's not your fault,' she said. 'You weren't to blame.'

'You can't really blame the child,' Ben said flatly, wondering if his voice was as rusty as it sounded. 'What are the injuries?'

Meg shot him a look. 'Only minor. Look, you can see the mark on his forehead where he hit the side window, and he's showing a few signs of concussion—sickness, headache, a little bit of dizziness, but nothing drastic.'

'Neck's clear, though,' Tom said, studying the X-rays, 'so we can take the neck brace off him now. He'll be much happier then, but I think we need to keep him in for twenty-four hours for observation just to be on the safe side. I'll arrange for his transfer to Paediatrics.'

The child was wheeled away, the tearful mother following with the older child in tow, and Ben turned to her and said angrily, 'How could you describe that child's injuries as minor and brush them aside? You see this sort of thing all the time—senseless, pointless injuries to innocent children. That could have been much worse, and the mother should be made to realise it. People should make more effort to discipline their children and keep them restrained. It really isn't fair—'

'It isn't fair to blame the mother either,' she retorted, and she glared at him.

'Of course it is! Who else? She's in charge of the children—'

'Do you have kids?' she asked bluntly, and he sucked in a breath.

'No.'

'So don't be in such a hurry to judge.'

He opened his mouth to reply, shut it again firmly before he said something he'd regret, and, yanking off his mike, he threw his clipboard down and stalked out.

Well, what on earth was that all about?

Meg stared after him, a part of her still furious, the other part frantically backtracking over the scene and their conversation to try and work out what exactly it was.

'What's flown up his skirt?' Pete said, and Steve shrugged.

'Dunno. Want to see it again?'

'What for? Ditch it—we can't use it. On second thoughts, save it for now. It might come in handy later—bit of emotional involvement. God knows, he's shown precious little of it.'

'You aren't supposed to get involved,' Meg said, wincing inwardly as she said it because she, of all people, had no room to criticise on that score. 'I'm going to find him.'

She walked out of the door, turned left and almost fell over him. He was standing there, staring out over the car park, a muscle jumping in his jaw.

'Ben?'

'Get off my case, Meg. I don't need you telling me how to behave.'

She stared at him. 'Excuse me, I thought you were telling me.'

'Oh, my God, it's Ben Maguire!'

'I'm getting out of here,' he muttered, and before she could say anything he was gone, striding across the car park, his long legs eating up the ground.

She hesitated, gnawing her lip while she debated following him. Then an ambulance turned into the hospital drive, lights flashing, and she sighed and went back in.

He was an adult. It was no skin off her nose if he abandoned the programme halfway through the second day's filming. In fact, it was a relief.

Pete and Steve were waiting, Rae busying herself with reassembling Ben's clipboard.

'Well?'

'He's gone. He walked off. I think he's gone to his car.'

'Damn. What the hell's eating him?' Pete growled, but she had no answers, either for him or for herself. Except that every time there was a child, every time it got a bit rough, every time they were in Resus—something to do with that combination was in some way connected with why he'd given up medicine, she was almost sure.

Not that she could ask, even if he'd been here, but if it had been a child who'd been injured, maybe that explained why he felt so strongly about the child's restraint, unwilling to absolve the parent of blame.

Shrugging it off, she tidied up the bed in Resus and readied it for the next patient. It was none of her business after all. If he didn't choose to tell her, she couldn't be expected to understand.

Pete was punching numbers into his mobile, and Meg covered his hand.

'You can't use that in here, Pete. You'll have to go outside.'

With a muttered oath he stalked off, and Steve shrugged and grinned at her.

'Well, if they're all going to mess off I might as well go and find some coffee. It's obviously going to be one of those days. Coming, Rae?'

Ben reappeared at twelve, almost three hours later, and stationed himself beside her.

'So what are you doing now?' he asked Meg, as if he'd just popped out for a coffee, and she flicked a disbelieving glance over him and turned back to the white board.

'Patient in three who's had a fall. She's got a leg ulcer, and she's banged it and damaged the skin. It needs dressing and then she can go home.'

She saw him relax—not much, just a slight shift of the muscles under his shirt, but enough to know that this, anyway, wasn't a threat. Good. She'd had enough of his histrionics for the day, whatever their cause. Thank God she had a day off tomorrow.

'Where are the others?'

'Staff room,' she said, and he disappeared and returned with them a minute later. Not long enough, certainly, for a Q and A session on the reason for his abrupt departure.

Not that it was any of her business, she reminded herself again. She went to see her patient, a regular with unsteady legs and a cheerful disposition, leaving them to follow.

'Hello, Annie, my darling, how are you?'

'Oh, Meg, hello, dear. I had another fall.'

'So I gather. That was silly. Annie, they're filming for the Ben Maguire show on the television. Are you OK for them to film you?'

'Does that mean I get interviewed by this handsome young man?' she asked, openly flirting with him, and to give him credit, he crouched down and flirted right back.

'I'll take that as a yes, then,' Rae said, grinning at Meg, and she nodded.

'I think so,' she replied, and watched them flirting with each other like teenagers.

And how! Ben was as charming as she'd ever seen him, and Annie loved it. So did Meg, because it made a painful procedure on a frail and elderly patient no more traumatic than putting a plaster on a little graze.

Endorphins, she thought. She's feeling special, and it's releasing a flood of feel-good hormones in her brain and taking her mind off it.

Meg thought she might as well not have been there, except for the dressing, and that suited her fine. She was already sick of answering silly questions and explaining what she was doing, and if Ben would only stop asking her, he'd find she'd give him the answers he wanted anyway, as a matter of course in her dealings with the patient. But Annie knew the score and, since she was busy with Ben, Meg decided to grab a few moments' peace and quiet.

Then Ben glanced up and said, 'Can you explain what you're doing?'

So much for her peace and quiet!

'Annie caught the tender skin on her ulcer when she fell,' she said, pointing out the messy tear so Steve could zoom in on it. 'I just need to clean it up, check there's no hidden damage and then dress it. The trouble is that venous ulcers, or ulcers that form because of poor blood supply, can be notoriously difficult to heal, and anything like this just sets it back, which is a shame.

And also, of course, there's the danger of infection with a dirty wound. Annie, what did you fall over, my love?'

'A shopping trolley—you know, one of those tartan bags on a stick that people drag round after themselves. I just didn't see it—very silly of me, I know. I hit myself on the corner of a shelf, I think.'

'So she's had quite a heavy fall, but inside a shop and there probably isn't much risk of infection. Before we send her home, though, we need to make sure she's not got any other injuries lurking that she may not have noticed or thought about.'

'Any other bumps?' Ben asked Annie, and she leant over confidingly.

'I'm not sure. I don't think so, but perhaps you'd better check me over!' she said, giggling like a schoolgirl.

Ben chuckled and patted her hand. 'You'll get me in trouble,' he said.

'Just so long as it isn't the other way round!' she said with a wicked little wink, and he laughed again and told her she was incorrigible.

He was being so nice to her, and while Meg cleaned the wound and dressed it and explained to the camera how the colloidal dressing worked, the other half of her mind—no, make that at least three quarters—was thinking what a crying shame it was he'd given up medicine, because his bedside manner, when he made the effort, was wonderful.

And she didn't want to think about his bedside manner, not while he was twinkling and flirting and giving Annie the benefit of that incredibly sexy smile.

'Right, my love, you're all finished,' she said briskly, and Annie looked blankly at her for a second.

'Oh!' She looked down at her leg and blinked in surprise. 'That was quick. Thank you, Meg, dear. It doesn't feel too bad either. Bit tender.'

'It will be. I've put another colloidal dressing on it and I'll put some Tubigrip on to support your whole leg for a while, just to keep the swelling down.'

She measured the bandage from toe to mid-thigh, doubled it and slipped it over the cylindrical frame, then slid it onto Annie's leg to give a smooth double layer with a nice snug fit.

'How's that?'

'Lovely. Now, I'd better pull my skirt down before I embarrass this nice young man by flashing my legs at him!' she twinkled, and Ben laughed, showing yet again this warm and human side of him she'd hardly seen before.

It was just a shame he couldn't seem to show it to her...

CHAPTER FIVE

'FLISS?'

'Meg, hi! How's it going?'

Meg tucked her feet under her and cradled the phone between her ear and shoulder while she peeled the top off a pot of yoghurt. 'OK, I suppose. Well, no, pretty grim really, if I'm honest. I'd love to see you. Are you busy tonight?'

'No, of course not. Want dinner?'

Meg didn't hesitate. The yoghurt was the only thing in her fridge that wasn't out of date or wrinkled, and she jumped at the chance of some of Fliss's wonderful home cooking.

'That would be great. What time?'

She never found out. Her phone beeped three times and died, and she stared at it in disbelief and stuck it back on the charger. Of course, if she'd done that in the first place, the battery wouldn't have been flat now, and her mobile was flat, too.

Oh, well, she thought with a shrug, Fliss won't mind if I'm early. I'll just go.

She eyed the yoghurt, thought of breakfast and put it back in the fridge, then grabbed her bag and keys and let herself out, running down the four flights of stairs to the street door.

That was the disadvantage of living on the top floor, she thought, eyeing her mangled car radio aerial in disgust. She was too far from the vandals to see and hear them. She'd only been home for two hours!

Oh, well. At least it wasn't the windscreen wipers this time, and she had a fair idea who it was. If she could only catch them…

She turned on the engine, turned off the crackling radio and went via the corner shop to pick up a box of chocolate truffles. Fliss and Tom always had wine in stock and knew far more about it than she did, and the garden was stuffed with flowers, but she didn't like to go empty-handed. Anyway, Fliss was as thin as a rake, despite moaning about losing her waist, so chocolates were fine.

She drove straight round to the back of the house, let herself in through the side gate into the walled garden and banged on the kitchen door. There was no reply, and as the door was open she went in, calling out to Fliss.

Nothing, but she could hear footsteps overhead in the flat, so she dropped the truffles on the kitchen table, went through the connecting door into the rear hall and ran up the back stairs.

'Fliss, hope I'm not too early but my phone cut out…' She trailed to a halt in confusion. 'Ben?'

Oh, yes, it was certainly Ben—stark naked and wringing wet, and as she stared a dribble ran from his hair and trailed down his broad, solid chest, through the scatter of dark hair and down, disappearing into the towel he held clamped firmly against the taut, smooth plane of his abdomen. Her eyes locked on it, mesmerised, and for a moment she forgot to breathe.

Forgot her own name, for heaven's sake, because he was simply…

A hand—the one that wasn't holding the towel—appeared in her line of sight, held flat at hip height, and he raised it slowly to his mocking eyes.

'Thank you,' he said, echoing her reaction at their first meeting, and she felt hot colour scorch her cheeks.

Gorgeous. He was simply, utterly gorgeous. Stunning. She gulped and sucked in some much-needed air. 'I'm sorry—I didn't realise you were here. I thought it was Fliss.'

'No, it's definitely me.' He looked down at himself and nodded confirmation. 'Yup, that's my body.'

She glanced down, her mouth forming an O, then yanked her eyes back up, her cheeks flaming again.

'So—how come...?'

'I'm staying here. The woman in the hotel got a bit much—like a black widow spider. I kept waiting for her to drag me into her lair and have her evil way with me.'

Oh, lord. Did he have to talk about that?

'Um—I'll let you get dressed,' she said, absurdly flustered considering she spent large parts of her day taking people's clothes off. But not this man's. Oh, no.

Unfortunately.

Quickly, before she could say or do anything else stupid, she turned and headed for the stairs, but his voice stopped her.

'Wait. They're out—they've gone to pick up the kids from Fliss's mother. Make yourself at home here, I won't be long. I want to talk to you.'

He did? That made a change. Maybe he was finally going to tell her what the hell was eating him.

With a shrug she headed for the sofa and stared resolutely out of the window, trying not to think about him dressing in the room next door, drying those long, muscular legs, rubbing a towel over them, over that flat, taut abdomen, the hair-scattered chest. Dragging on underwear, jeans, a shirt, clinging to the damp skin...

Damp? Try wet. He reappeared in moments, dressed in those disreputable old jeans again with a raspberry-pink T-shirt that was only slightly more respectable. She imagined it had once been red, but no more. A million washes had seen to that. And now there were damp patches appearing on it where the hair lay on his chest, moisture clinging to the curls. She could just picture it...

His feet were bare, and she could see the water gleaming on them as he walked round and stood in front of her, staring down at her in thoughtful silence.

She leant back against the sofa so she could look up at him without getting a crick in her neck, and after a while he sighed and scrubbed his hands through his hair.

'I owe you an apology,' he said eventually. 'I went off on one today, and I shouldn't have done. I'm sorry.'

Whatever she'd expected, it hadn't been that, and her jaw must have dropped, because he gave a short huff of laughter.

'Close your mouth, Meg,' he said gently.

It snapped shut, and she struggled upright, hitching herself into the corner of the sofa and crossing her legs, her hands tucked down under her ankles. He grinned crookedly.

'Michael sits like that,' he said softly, and dropped onto the other end of the sofa with a tired sigh.

She dragged in a breath and searched his face, but there were no clues. She let it out in a whoosh.

'So what brought that on?' she asked.

'The apology? My sense of justice, I suppose. It was hardly your fault. It just makes me angry when kids get injured needlessly.'

Meg nodded, knowing exactly where he was coming

from. 'You're absolutely right, of course. Parents should make every attempt to ensure their children are safe, but I didn't feel that that woman at that precise moment needed a lecture, and she has a point. Kids can make Houdini look like an amateur.'

Ben nodded. 'I know,' he said gruffly. 'Anyway, I'm sorry I laid into you and stalked off like that.'

Conceding the point *and* apologising? Wow. Tipping her head, she asked, 'So where did you go?'

He shrugged and shook his head. 'Dunno. There's a park somewhere near the hospital. I went for a run, then found a café and got a coffee, then gave in to my conscience and went back.'

'So can I ask why you overreacted?' she said softly, but his mouth tightened into a grim line.

'Let's just say today was too close for comfort.'

So Meg let it go. For now.

'Oh, well, you get a day off tomorrow,' she reminded him, but he shook his head.

'No. I'm shadowing you on and off duty for a week. That's the deal, although it doesn't make you any happier than it makes me. As you said, we're stuck with each other.'

Did her dismay show on her face? She hoped not. 'The viewers will die of boredom. I need to do something to my flat, because it's a bit of a pigsty at the moment, and the only thing in my fridge is a yoghurt, so it's not going to be exactly riveting.'

'Or we could skive,' he said slowly.

'Skive?'

'As in bunk off—play truant—run away?'

The idea had definite appeal, and it certainly beat doing her washing in public! 'Where did you have in mind?'

He gave a deep grunt of laughter. 'Somewhere Pete Harrison can't find us,' he said drily.

'Alaska?' she suggested, and he chuckled.

'Bit chilly. How about a walk on the beach?'

'There's a place near Southwold,' she suggested. 'It's pretty empty. There's not a lot goes on there, just a few holiday cottages and the gulls for company. You'll get some privacy, especially if we go early in the morning.'

She half expected him to baulk at that, but he didn't.

'We could go for a run—is it sandy?'

She nodded slowly. 'Yes. There's a shingle bank at the top, but it's lovely by the water—firm and smooth.'

'Then we'll do that. I'll pick you up. We'll go at five, before Pete starts to nag, and we'll get breakfast somewhere on the way back, and then, if they really insist, they can follow us for the rest of the day while you do your shopping.'

Meg rolled her eyes. 'Oh, joy,' she said, but all she could think about was running on the beach with him in less than twelve hours, and her heart gave a little jiggle.

'This is gorgeous.'

She smiled. 'I'm glad you like it. It's one of my favourite places in the world.'

'And my mobile's not about to ring, so no Pete to nag us.'

'What a shame.'

He returned her grin, and waved a hand at the beach. 'OK, lead the way.'

She set off along the sand, the wind tugging at her hair and Ben beside her, easily keeping pace, measuring his stride to hers. And it was heaven. The sun was crawling slowly up into the sky, its early rays not yet too hot for comfort, and the beach was utterly deserted.

She flashed him a smile, and he smiled back, looking utterly relaxed for the first time that week. Relaxed and happy, and because of that she relaxed too, and filled her lungs with the fresh sea air, and stopped thinking.

Stopped thinking about Ben, and whatever it was about the hospital that made him so uncomfortable, and why he'd given up medicine, and concentrated instead on putting one foot in front of the other and enjoying his company in the glorious dawn.

And then, of course, because nothing lasted for ever, they reached the end of the long stretch of beach and slowed to a walk.

He turned to her, hands on hips and breathing fast, and grinned. 'What now?'

She grinned back and shrugged. 'Up to you. We can run back, we can walk back—'

'Or we could go for a swim.'

'I haven't got my bikini.'

'Neither have I.'

His mouth twitched, and she bit her lip.

'Are you suggesting we skinny-dip?' she asked, and he gave one of those Gallic shrugs that turned her heart inside out.

'I had thought of underwear. We can always go commando on the way home. But skinny-dipping's cool by me.'

She looked around. Nothing. Not even the dog walkers were out yet. She mentally scanned her underwear and could have groaned. Because they were running, she'd put on her sports bra and proper knickers—hardly the sexiest things in the world, and certainly nothing she'd want to show off to Ben.

But they knocked spots off removing everything completely!

'I promise I won't look,' he said, but his eyes were full of mischief and she didn't believe him for a moment.

And suddenly she decided she didn't care. It was a gorgeous morning, there wasn't a soul around, and if she wanted to swim naked with the sexiest and most intriguing man she'd ever met, there was nothing to stop her.

Except cowardice.

'Race you,' she said. Ripping off her T-shirt and shorts, she kicked off her trainers, tugged off her socks and pelted for the sea.

'Fraidy cat,' he yelled, racing past her clad in a pair of clingy jersey boxers and diving cleanly into the waves.

Maybe, but she wasn't ready to bare all in front of him, sexy and intriguing or not, and it seemed she wasn't alone.

She hit the water less than a second after him, and the cold took her breath away.

She shrieked as she came up for air, and he laughed and dived under the surface, coming up behind her, sluicing the water off his hair and shaking his head like a dog. She turned and splashed him, and the next minute they were playing like dolphins, diving and twisting and laughing, always laughing, until finally they came to a halt, just inches apart.

Their eyes locked, and she felt her smile fade.

'You've got hair in your eyes,' he murmured, and his hand came out and lifted a wet strand away from her face. For one breathless, endless moment she thought he was going to kiss her, and her heart stopped.

Then he turned away, diving into the water and swimming strongly out to sea, leaving her treading water and watching him carve his way through the waves as if he'd been born there, while her heart hiccuped and started to beat again.

Her hand came up and covered her lips, tingling with anticipation. She'd really thought he was going to kiss her. Could have sworn it. She ached for his touch—ached to hold him, to be held by him.

But it wasn't to be, apparently.

With a weary sigh she turned, making her way slowly through the shallows to the firm, wet sand of the beach. Without looking back, she tugged on her T-shirt and shorts, then stuffed her socks into her shoes and moved up onto the dry sand. She was cold now, and she sat hugging her legs and shivering as she watched him make his way slowly back to shore.

Ben dressed in silence, then came and stood over her, holding out his hand without a word. She let him pull her to her feet, and without releasing her he turned and headed slowly back the way they'd come.

They strolled in silence, although not really a companionable silence. It was too full of anticipation to be simply companionable, and Meg felt the tug of attraction between them humming with tension as they walked.

Was this the beginning of something between them? Or just a truce? She didn't know, but the question burned in her mind as they walked along the water's edge, their bare feet leaving imprints in the wet sand.

At regular intervals along the shoreline the remains of the old wooden breakwaters marched out into the sea, sticking up like rows of black and broken teeth out of the sand, and beyond one there was a drop.

He jumped down, turned and lifted her, sliding her down his body so she could feel every inch of him. His hands had slipped up her ribcage to come to a halt under her breasts, and as he set her on her feet his eyes locked with hers. For a moment he hesitated, then released her and turned away.

She bit back a sigh of frustration and fell in beside him. So, just a truce, then. Well, if he wouldn't kiss her, maybe he would talk. Open up a bit, reveal something of himself—anything! She was getting sick of knowing so little, and he intrigued her. Boy, did he intrigue her! She tried to keep her voice casual.

'So how did a nice guy like you end up in a place like this?' she said, and he chuckled.

'Is Suffolk so bad?'

'I meant the TV thing. It's a bit off the wall.'

He shrugged. 'I'd done a bit of TV doctor stuff—nothing significant, but I had contacts. I needed a job—they were looking for a lunatic to take on the show and I fitted the bill.'

She chuckled. 'A lunatic?'

'Some of the things I've done have been a bit crazy. A bit dangerous.'

'Mmm. This is a bit tame for you, really, isn't it, shadowing me?'

'Tame? I wouldn't call it tame. Just…different.'

'So,' she said, feeling her heart pump a little and trying hard to keep her voice casual, 'what branch of medicine were you in?'

For a moment she thought he wouldn't reply, but then he did, to her surprise. 'Anaesthetics. I was specialising in paeds.'

'Whereabouts? Town, city, country?'

'The Royal London.'

'Wow. That's a bit cutting edge—lots of trauma. Anything to do with why you gave up?'

'I don't want to talk about it.'

Too far. 'OK,' she demurred. Well, almost. 'Just one more thing.'

'What?' His voice was flat and uninviting now, but she persevered.

'Were you struck off?'

He stopped dead in his tracks and turned to stare at her in amazement. 'Str— No, I most certainly was not struck off!'

She lifted her hands in surrender. 'Just asking.'

'Well, don't,' he growled. 'It's none of your damn business.'

It wasn't, of course, but...

She let her breath out on a gusty sigh. 'I'm sorry. I wasn't really being nosy. I just thought it might help me understand you a little better. I'm not Pete, you know. I don't have an axe to grind, and I don't want to do this programme any more than you do. I just thought you might like to know you had a friend.'

He grunted. He didn't sound convinced, but he turned and started walking again as if nothing had happened. If she hadn't seen the shutter come down over his eyes she might have believed him.

So. Paediatric anaesthetics at the Royal London. Burn-out? It happened at major trauma centres, and with HEMS, the helicopter emergency medical service, being based there, it was certainly one of the major trauma centres for the London area, especially for RTAs, since they covered the M25 and all areas within it, and the M25 was the busiest motorway in England and suffered in consequence with more than its share of accidents.

Was that it? Just too much? Too many senseless RTA

victims? Maybe a child who hadn't been restrained—maybe several, over and over again, because it happened, he was right, and there wasn't really any excuse that training couldn't overcome unless the child had learning difficulties of some sort.

Oh, it was a minefield, the clues too deeply hidden for her to spot them all, but at least she was a little nearer to understanding him. She hoped.

They walked in silence now, but a different kind of silence, and the gap between them could have been a mile wide. Certainly their hands were no longer linked, and she missed the warmth of that contact more than she'd believed possible.

Crazy. She was getting in too deep, getting too involved with a man who wanted nothing to do with her.

Except he had so nearly kissed her.

'What's that?'

He'd stopped, his head raised, listening, but over the breeze off the sea and the lapping of the waves she could hear only the gulls wheeling overhead, their keening cries strangely bleak now.

And then she heard it—a cry for help, someone screaming, sobbing, and without hesitation she broke into a run. Ben streaked away from her, his longs legs eating up the sand, and moments later she saw them.

They were by one of the breakwaters, two girls crouched down low. One seemed to be holding the other one up somehow and sobbing frantically.

'She's stuck on a spike!' she screamed. 'She slipped and fell—help me!'

And then Ben was there on one knee, taking the weight of the injured girl in his arms, propping her on his other leg, taking over. As Meg arrived, his eyes met hers and the message in them wasn't one she wanted to read.

'It's OK, I've got you,' he was saying reassuringly, but Meg wasn't sure if he was talking to the girl who was impaled or the other one, hovering beside him, tears streaming down her face.

'We need an ambulance,' she sobbed. 'A doctor.'

'I'm a doctor, and she's a nurse,' Ben said in a voice designed to give them confidence, and Meg's breath caught. Thank God. She'd been so afraid she'd have to do this alone, but to her relief he was no longer denying his medical background.

He turned to Meg. 'She's caught on something,' he said softly. 'Could you look?'

She ducked down round him and peered up, but it was hard to see. The light jacket the injured girl was wearing was drooping down and obstructing her view, and as Meg pushed it out of the way blood ran through a tear in the cloth and splashed all over her.

'We've got a bit of a bleed here, Ben,' she said calmly, hoping he would pick up on her meaning without terrifying the other girl. 'And a definite impalement—something's sticking into her side, but I have no idea how long it is.'

'OK,' he said calmly. 'Can you see what it is?'

'Not really.'

The other girl was whimpering, her voice high and out of control now, almost unintelligible with fear. 'Help her. Please, help her—she's my sister.'

'It's OK, my love,' Meg said, squeezing her hand. 'What's your name?'

'Kate—I'm…Kate, and she's…Jess.'

'OK, Kate, have you got a mobile?' Ben asked urgently, and the girl who'd spoken nodded.

'Yes. I'll ring—who?'

'Nine-nine-nine. You'll need ambulance, paramedic, fire brigade to free her—'

'Ben, she'll need airlifting,' Meg advised, watching the blood drip into the water. Water. Dear God.

They were kneeling in water, and the tide was coming in, racing across the almost flat sand of the beach, advancing at a terrifying rate. They had five, maybe ten minutes before the water would start to slosh against Jess's wound, and another ten before she was underwater.

'Ben, we're running out of time,' she said under her breath, and he nodded.

'There's no sign of anything coming through this side. Can you see what's holding her? It might not be very long.'

She looked again. 'Metal. A narrow metal plate on the side of the post.' Rusty and filthy and encrusted with weed, and no clue how long it was, how far it had penetrated. Dear God. And the tide was rising inch by inch.

'Make a pack out of something—your T-shirt'll do. And press it firmly all round the wound, holding it tight.'

But she'd already done it by the time he'd finished talking. Anchoring it with one hand, she held the other hand out to Kate.

'Give me the phone, I'll talk to them. You hold this, and don't let go.'

She moved away from Ben and the girls, speaking to the operator at the ambulance headquarters. 'We need the air ambulance, as fast as you can. We've got an impaled casualty on the water-line and the tide's coming in fast. We'll need the fire brigade with cutting gear, too.' Giving swift, accurate directions, she checked they'd understood and then called Tom to warn him.

'OK. You say she's impaled, so there's no way you can lift her off, not if she's bleeding. Check her pulse.'

She stuck the phone under her ear and reached for Jess's neck. 'Weak, rapid, thready,' she reported, as much to Ben as to Tom. 'Resps are harsh and guarded. She's a bit cyanotic.'

'Damn. What's Ben doing?'

'Holding her up. He's got his hands full.'

'Is he OK?'

She glanced at him, and saw the concentration in his face. He was talking to Jess, soothing her, although Meg wasn't sure she could hear.

'For now,' she confirmed.

'Right. Get him to hold her as still as possible, and try and get a pressure pad on the wound.'

'Done that. Tom—the tide. We haven't got long.'

'Save the phone battery. I'll hassle them. You look out for the chopper,' he said, and rang off.

She handed the phone back to Kate.

'Well? Are they coming?'

'They're coming.'

'But the water—'

'It's OK, Kate. It'll be OK, they'll be here in a couple of minutes,' she said, injecting as much reassurance as she could into her voice. 'Ten minutes, tops. Ben, Tom says leave her there but hold her as steady as you can.'

He nodded. 'I am. Keep pressing that pad. If we can slow the bleeding…'

He broke off, shifting his grip slightly, and the water swirled in around him and splashed against the wooden barrier, drenching them and flowing away bright red.

Their eyes locked. Time was running out.

'She's going to die,' Kate sobbed. 'Jess, please, please, don't die!'

The cold water had roused Jess, and her eyes flickered open. 'Kate,' she said weakly. 'Hurts. Want Mum.'

'Hold her hand,' Meg said, and Kate knelt down on the other side, on the higher sand, and clutched her sister's hand for dear life. It suddenly dawned on Meg that they were probably too young to be staying in the area alone, and in that case…

'Are your parents near here?' she asked, and Kate nodded.

'In that cottage over there.' She jerked her head towards the road, and in the distance Meg could see a little white weatherboard beach house. 'We're on holiday.'

'Call them. They need to know.'

While she fumbled with the phone and spoke frantically to her parents, Meg watched the water rise faster than she would have believed possible.

'They're coming,' Kate said, and looked at the water, her eyes widening as she realised just how quickly the tide was coming in. 'Can't you lift her off? She'll drown… Oh, God, help her, please!'

'Bleeding's eased,' Meg told Ben, but they both knew it was probably because the exit was obstructed and the wound was probably still bleeding inside her chest.

'Could be an intercostal vessel,' Ben said, obviously reading her mind. And that, of course, was the best possible scenario. Meg could only hope Jess was that lucky, because if not they were going to lose her.

Another wave came, higher this time, and Meg did her best to block it so it broke against her and not the wood, but it swirled round, of course, and this time it didn't recede nearly so far. Jess's legs were lying in it, her hair trailed in it, and the next wave was right up against her back, soaking the T-shirt Meg was using as a pressure pad and rendering it useless.

Then Ben went still.

'Chopper,' he said shortly, and met Meg's eyes again as the water swirled even higher and flooded over Jess's chest. 'I'm going to lift her off. We don't have time to wait for the fire brigade to cut her free. If we don't get her off we'll risk sea water pouring into the chest wound, and we've got back-up now. Kate, go and wave and attract their attention,' he ordered, and Kate leapt to her feet and ran up the beach, screaming and waving her arms frantically as the yellow dot of the East Anglian Air Ambulance zeroed in on them.

'Right. That's her out of the way. This may not be nice,' Ben said tightly. 'I want you to get down there and see what's happening as I lift her, and be ready to press something over it the moment she's free. At the very least she'll have a sucking chest wound. I don't want to think about other scenarios.'

Neither did Meg. She waited for the water to recede, then took away the pressure pad and nodded. 'OK. Lift away.'

Her heart was pounding, but the lift was clean, and the metal blade had only penetrated a couple of inches. She pressed the T-shirt back over the hole and ran with Ben up the beach, setting Jess down on her side with the wound upwards, away from the sand, just as her parents arrived, her father in pyjamas, her mother in shorts and a nightshirt, both of them frantic.

'Jess!' the mother screamed, but the father held her back, giving them room.

Then the air ambulance team were there, two paramedics and all the equipment, covering the gaping chest wound with a plastic sheet taped on three sides to allow air trapped in the chest to escape, giving her oxygen, getting in an IV line.

By this time the police had also arrived, a WPC taking Jess's shaking mother in her arms and hugging her reassuringly while her father hugged Kate, falling apart completely now her parents were there and it was all right to give in.

Then Jess was loaded and away, her mother at her side, and the police were taking the rest of the family to the hospital by car. 'They'll be there in about five minutes,' Meg told Ben, watching them leave. Then she turned to him and saw the bleak expression on his face.

'I shouldn't have lifted her, but I had no choice. She would have drowned before we could have cut that metal bar. I hope to God she makes it.'

'She stands far more chance because of what we did than if we hadn't been here,' she pointed out, but his mouth was grim and he didn't look convinced.

He was shaking, shaking like she was, all over, from adrenaline and cold. The sun wasn't hot yet, and they were soaked and chilled through from the sea water.

And she was standing there in her bra and shorts, covered in blood, when the fire brigade arrived.

Great. All those hunky firemen catching her in her bloody underwear—literally—with her nipples standing out like chapel hat pegs and her skin as bumpy as the Christmas goose.

Someone put a blanket round her shoulders, and she and Ben were led along the beach to the car park. They'd lost their shoes, washed away by the incoming tide, but she didn't care.

'We'll be fine now,' Ben said. 'We've got fresh

clothes in the car. To be honest, all we really need is a hot shower.'

So the firemen left them to it, and Ben threw her a thick, warm sweater out of the back of his car.

'Here, put this on,' he instructed, but she didn't need telling twice. She was cold and nearly naked, and she snuggled gratefully into it.

'What about you?' she asked, her teeth chattering, but he just grunted.

'I'll be fine. I'll put the heater on. Get in.'

'I'm covered in blood and sand and sea water. What about your car?'

'What about my car? The leather will wipe clean, and even if it won't, I don't see us walking home.'

No. Silly. So she got in, and within moments the heat started to filter through the vents and she began to relax.

'So much for my day off,' she said drily.

'So much for our breakfast.'

'I'll cook you brunch,' she said, and his mouth tightened. 'I can cook, you know, I won't poison you.'

'I'm sure. I'm just not hungry.'

She looked more keenly at him, taking in the lines of strain around his eyes, the grim set of his mouth, and wondered how much of an ordeal that morning had been to him.

She still had no idea what had happened in his past, but this morning he'd done what had been necessary and coped with the crisis without a second's hesitation. Yet now it was over he was retreating again, disappearing off into that private world that had KEEP OUT! written on it in letters ten feet high.

And she was definitely on the outside.

CHAPTER SIX

OF COURSE the phone wasn't quiet for many moments. That would have been too much to expect, and if he'd had a grain of sense he would have turned it off.

With a growl of frustration Ben punched a button on the handset, and, because it was hands-free, Meg also got the benefit of Pete's wrath firsthand.

'What the hell's going on, Maguire? And where's the nurse? We're supposed to be with her and you've buggered off somewhere, and we went to the hospital to see if anyone had any idea where you were, since you've seen fit to check out of the hotel without discussing it with me, and all hell was breaking loose, a girl brought in by air ambulance and they said you and Meg been involved in some dramatic rescue.'

'News travels fast,' Ben said drily, and Pete exploded.

'What? It's true? So where are you? And why, for God's sake, don't you answer your phone?'

'Because we've been for a run on the beach. That's what we were doing when we found her injured.'

'Well, get yourselves back here, fast. If you'd been here we could have followed it, but instead—'

'If we'd been there,' he said tightly, 'you wouldn't have a story to cover because she would have been brought in dead and we would have known nothing about it. And anyway, why the hell should we want to come to the hospital? It's Meg's day off.'

'The parents want to see you—to thank you. So get

your butts over here now and start earning that exorbitant salary.'

'I wish,' Ben muttered. Stabbing the phone with his index finger, he cut the producer off in midstream.

Meg stared at him in astonishment. 'Is he always like that?'

'Only if he feels a photo opportunity slipping through his fingers.' He sighed roughly. 'I'm sorry about that.'

'Don't worry. So, are we?'

'Are we what?'

'Going to the hospital?'

He met her eyes briefly, then looked back at the road. 'Do you want to?'

'I wouldn't mind. Not for Pete, and certainly not to be thanked, but just to see if Jess is all right and give Kate a hug. Poor girl was distraught. She could only have been—what, fourteen? Fifteen?'

He shrugged. 'Search me. They looked about the same age. Twins?'

'Could be. So, are we going?'

He sighed and scrubbed a hand through his hair. 'Not without a shower. I stink of seaweed and I've got dried blood under my nails, and Pete will have Steve hovering there with the camera. But, yes, if you want, we can go. I should be filming with you today anyway, and it will make good TV, so let's do it and keep Pete happy.'

'The line of least resistance?' Meg said with a smile, and he gave a hollow laugh.

'Something like that. Want me to drop you off and wait for you while you shower, or pick you up later?'

'I've got clothes with me to change into—why don't we go straight to Tom and Fliss's and shower there, to save time?'

Because I don't want you naked in my flat, he

thought, and then had to shut his eyes for a heartbeat because that was such a downright lie. He did want her naked—naked and writhing under him, with those full, firm breasts unleashed from that awful, sexless and bloodstained sports bra and spilling eagerly into his hands…

'Ben? Where's the fire?'

He eased his foot off the accelerator and sucked in a lungful of air. 'Sorry,' he muttered, and spent the next ten minutes forcing himself to concentrate.

She'd meant to use Fliss's shower, but when they got back there Fliss was out and she had no choice but to use Ben's.

'You go first,' he said, and so she went into his bathroom, amongst all his toiletries, and discovered that he didn't put the lid on his toothpaste and squeezed the tube in the middle and didn't rinse the basin, so there were little tiny dark hairs all round it from when he'd shaved.

But he used proper shampoo, and soap the same as his horribly expensive aftershave, so that when she'd washed herself she smelt of him.

And then he was banging on the door and telling her to hurry up, and she dragged the towel he'd given her round her still-wet body, scooped up her clothes and opened the door.

'All yours,' she said with a bright smile, and he growled something under his breath and shot past her.

She dressed quickly and rubbed her hair dry with the towel, then spent the next five minutes trying to get the tangles out of it because he hadn't had any conditioner, of course. And then he was there, dressed in decent jeans—for once—and a shirt left open at the neck, with the cuffs turned back to expose those lean, tanned forearms with the scatter of dark hair that sent shivers up her spine.

He was fastening his watch, the slim steel bracelet businesslike and not in the least showy, and she suddenly realised just how simple his tastes were, clean and economical, nothing flashy.

Even his car was just a straightforward saloon, nothing out of the ordinary, nothing to attract attention apart from the fact that it whispered quality.

'All set?' he asked, and she nodded.

'Hair's still damp, but it'll be dry by the time we get there. I don't suppose you've got a hair-dryer?'

'There's one in the bedroom,' he said, and produced it. 'Courtesy of Fliss,' he explained, and she ran it quickly over her hair, taking off the worst of the dampness, and then they headed to the hospital.

Pete pounced on them, and not for the first time Meg wondered how Ben coped with him and hadn't simply landed him one by now on his arrogant and bossy nose.

Tom caught up with them in A and E, and for their benefit and that of the camera explained what they'd done to Jess when she'd been brought in.

'She'd got a sucking chest wound, of course—so when she tried to breathe in, air was dragged into her chest through the hole, instead of into her lungs through her windpipe, so her oxygen saturation was very low. On top of that she had severe bleeding from the entry wound, but that was just a blood vessel serving the muscles between the ribs, and nothing major. It doesn't look like she got too much sea water in the wound. She's had surgery, and I gather she's in Recovery, and her parents are waiting to thank you both.'

'And her sister? Did anybody look at her? She was very shocked,' Meg pointed out, and Tom nodded.

'She got quickly checked over but she was fine, just needed to know her sister was going to be all right. So you two are the heroes of the hour, and as far as that family are concerned you could walk on water, so you'd better go and claim your fame.'

Ben grunted. 'That's absolutely the last thing I want to do,' he began, but Tom shook his head.

'You have to go. This isn't about you, it's about two people whose daughter nearly died, who want to thank you for saving her life. That's all. They know about the camera, they're quite happy, so go and be gracious.'

'Yes, boss,' Ben said, shooting Tom a crooked grin, and with a sigh he rested his hand on the small of Meg's back and ushered her forwards.

'Lead on, then,' he said, and she took them up to the cardiothoracic theatre suite and found Jess's family sitting at her bedside in Recovery.

'I'd better just OK it,' Meg said before they went in, and spoke briefly to the senior nurse.

'Oh, the heroes!' she said with a grin. 'Sure, but don't be long. We haven't got anyone else in here at the moment, but we've got another patient coming out of Theatre in a few minutes, and we're moving Jess to the ward in a little while, so keep it brief.'

'Will do,' Meg promised, and, giving the others the nod, she made her way over to the bed. 'Hi, there,' she murmured, and Kate looked up and leapt to her feet.

'Meg!' she cried, and Meg opened her arms and hugged her slender little frame.

'How are you? Are you OK?'

'I'm fine,' she said shakily. 'Jess is going to be OK. Thank you so, so much...'

And she started to laugh and cry at the same time, so Meg hugged her again, rocking her and patting her back and letting her get it out of her system. When she looked up, Ben's hand was being almost wrung off by Kate and Jess's father, and their mother was clinging to his other hand and looking distinctly tearful as well.

'It wasn't me,' Ben was saying. 'I just held her. Meg did all the briefing of the emergency services and put the pressure pad on the wound and kept an eye on her condition. I just held her still—took her weight.'

'And made a very brave decision, I gather.'

He looked at her father. 'Not really. It was risk injuring her further, or leave her there and let her drown. It was a no-brainer, really. She was just very, very lucky.'

They nodded, and the father swallowed hard.

'She's been ill—we've nearly lost her a couple of times—but we've got her through it and she's turned the corner and made it to her sixteenth birthday, and to lose her now, after all that, well, I don't think we could have survived it—any of us. Especially Kate. They're very close, being twins, even though they're not identical.'

'I'm only surprised you were up that early,' Ben teased, turning to Kate, and she smiled ruefully.

'Not my idea. Jess's got this thing about the dawn. Every one is another victory, she says, and she loves to be out there, watching the sun come up. I don't mind in the winter, but in the summer it can be a bit early!'

Meg chuckled, but Ben's laugh sounded rusty, and she glanced up and, for the briefest instant before he shuttered them, caught the pain in his eyes.

And then Jess stirred, mumbling something, and their attention was distracted, and by the time Meg looked at

him again his face was back under control and his eyes
were carefully blank.

'OK, guys, we'll leave you in peace now,' he murmured, and with another round of thanks they escaped,
trailing Pete and Steve behind them. As the doors hissed
shut, Ben turned to Steve and said, 'OK, switch it off
now, that's enough of the damned heroics. Pete's got
what he wants.'

'No. Pete wants you following Meg doing what she
does on her day off,' Pete reminded him, and he sighed
and scrubbed a hand through his hair.

'Meg?' he said tiredly, and she took the hint.

'Well, I don't know about Ben, but I had an early
and dramatic start this morning, and I wouldn't mind a
quick kip. How about we reconvene at, say—two-
thirty?'

Pete opened his mouth, looked at her, then Ben, then
shut it and nodded. 'Fine. We'll do that. Your house?'

'My flat's a tip. How about the supermarket?'

Pete frowned. 'Is that the best you can do?'

'You want reality or something totally artificial? I
have nothing to eat in the place. I have no clean clothes.
You want to watch me, fine. It's the supermarket or the
laundrette. Take your pick. Ben, can we go?'

'Supermarket,' Pete said hastily. 'At least we can
look in your trolley, which is more than we can do with
the laundry basket. Which supermarket?'

She told him, talking over her shoulder as they
walked briskly down the corridor and out into the bless-
edly fresh air.

'Two-thirty,' Pete yelled after them, and Ben lifted
his hand and waved.

Or gestured? She didn't see, but he was chuckling,

and she was pleased to see him in a lighter frame of mind.

'So—what are we really doing?' he asked, and she frowned in puzzlement.

'I thought you wanted to get away.'

'I did—from them. Not necessarily from you. And we still haven't had breakfast,' he reminded her.

And so they did just that. They went to a place that sold all-day breakfasts, and had the full works, and didn't talk about medicine or the programme or what had happened that morning.

In fact, afterwards Meg had no idea what they had talked about. She just knew that by the time they turned up at the supermarket they were half an hour late and Pete was ripping his hair out.

'Sorry,' she lied blithely, 'I overslept. Right. Shall we shop?'

Doing her duty to the public and to the programme on her day off should have left Meg tired and unrefreshed.

Nope. She felt vital and alive, and sure as tooting it wasn't because of Pete's charm or her thoroughly unhealthy high-cholesterol brunch! The only thing she could put it down to was Ben. Being with him, working alongside him on Jess—just being around him was enough, but in the few brief moments after they'd lifted Jess off the metal spike before she'd been whisked away, she'd watched him working on her, and she'd got a glimpse of the doctor he tried so hard to deny.

And without the film crew there hanging on their every word, she seemed to be making progress. OK, the KEEP OUT sign was still hanging around, but every now and again the door blew open a crack and she got a glimpse of the real man.

The man she was falling in love with, hook, line and sinker.

'Oh, damn.'

She plopped down onto the bed and stared at herself in her mirror. 'Oh, Meg, you fool! He's going back to London in four days, you'll never see him again.'

Oh, no, that wasn't true. She would see him—see both of them, trapped for ever by the programme, their every movement documented for posterity.

Would it show? Was she to be seen gazing star-struck at him? No. Most probably glaring at him and hissing sparks. She seemed to save the star-struck for her off-camera moments and her dreams.

'Oh, damn,' she said again, and, hitching herself off the bed, she finished pulling on her running gear and made her way to the kitchen. A noise outside attracted her attention. Leaning over the sink, she peered down into the car park to see a group of youths kicking beer cans around.

They were obviously drunk or worse, and as she watched one of them reeled against her car and grabbed the aerial. OK, it was broken anyway, but then he reached for the windscreen wiper and she saw red.

Grabbing her keys, and her phone as an afterthought, she ran out of her flat, slamming the door and throwing herself down the stairs and out of the rear door.

'What the hell do you think you're doing?' she yelled, and they stopped and turned to her.

All of them. About six or seven of them, bigger than she'd realised, much drunker than she would have expected at five-thirty in the morning because they'd presumably been drinking all night and popping goodness knows what else besides. Slowly, their faces menacing, they moved towards her.

'Well, now, what have we here, boys? Oh, yes. Very nice. Cute little shorts, too.'

Damn. Damn, damn, damn.

She was wearing the little sleeveless vest top she used for jogging, and she shoved her hands into the front pocket casually, groping for her phone without taking her eyes off them.

Who on earth had she called last? And was her phone locked? Please, no. Let it have been Fliss. She'd call the police.

'What do you think you're doing to my car?' she said clearly. 'I come out of my home and find you vandalising my possessions, and I can't tell you how mad that makes me.'

'Oh, boys, watch yourselves, she's mad at us!' the one who'd spoken before jeered, and they all laughed and moved a little closer, closing in behind their spokesman.

So he was the ringleader. OK. She met his eyes squarely.

'OK, here's the deal,' she said, keeping her voice good and loud and desperately hoping all the button-pressing had connected with someone. 'I don't know who you are, I don't recognise you, and there's nobody but me to witness this. If you go now, and leave me and my car alone, I won't do any more about it. But if you take so much as one step nearer to me, I'll scream the place down, and all the people in my apartment building will come out and see you, and call the police, and you'll be in deep—'

She didn't even see him move. One second she was talking, the next she felt a searing pain in her side. She gasped with pain, but then everything went dark and she crumpled to the ground.

* * *

'Meg?'

Ben stared at the phone, held it to his ear and was about to ring off when he heard her talking. Her voice was muffled, but she seemed to be reasoning with someone, talking about nobody else witnessing something…

'Meg? Meg!' he yelled, and then there was a gasp and a roar of crackles and white noise, and the phone cut off.

'Dear God—Meg.' Ramming his feet into his shoes, he headed for the stairs, dialling 999 as he ran, then realised he didn't know Meg's address, just the way, because he'd picked her up the day before. He gave them Tom and Fliss's number to get directions, because by then he was in his car and speeding towards her flat, his heart hammering in his throat.

He had no idea what was going on, he just knew she was in trouble and he had to be there. She'd rung him. He was all she had, and he couldn't let her down.

He skidded to a halt into the car park and leapt out, looking around wildly for any sign of her, but there was nothing.

'Meg?' he yelled. 'Meg, where are you?'

And then he went round the corner of the building and saw her, lying propped up against the wall in the angle by a door, her eyes dazed with shock.

'Ben?' she said, and then she started to cry.

His first reaction was relief—relief that she was alive, that she was talking, that she recognised him. His second was a towering, furious rage at whoever had done this to her.

'It's OK, Meg. I'm here. You'll be all right.'

And gently, so as to not hurt her, he gathered her into his arms and held her trembling body close.

'Bastards,' she spat, and he lifted his head and looked down at her. Even in tears she was still furious, and he laughed with relief and shushed her.

Then the police were there, and Tom, and they were threatening to call an ambulance.

'I don't need an ambulance because some little scally threw a punch at me,' she muttered, and looked up at Ben, her face puzzled.

'How did you know?' she asked.

'You rang my phone. I could hear you.'

'I thought I rang Fliss. I just pressed call twice. I've never rung you.'

'You put my number in your phone yesterday evening and called it to check it was correct.'

She nodded. 'I did. I forgot. I'm sorry. I didn't mean to disturb you…'

He said something rude and sat back on his heels. 'Can you stand?'

'I don't know.'

He and Tom helped her carefully to her feet.

'OK?'

'I'll live. It hurts when I breathe in, but it's just bruising. I'll be all right. My phone's broken, though. I think I fell on it when he hit me.'

Ben huffed under his breath, and Tom shook his head.

'You need to go to hospital.'

'I do. To work.'

Tom swore softly and shook his head again. 'I don't think so. At least let me look at you—'

'Back off. If I need a big brother I'll ask for one,' she told him, and he shrugged and let it go.

Ben didn't. He didn't say anything, because the police were talking to her, but as far as he was concerned the topic was far from dead and buried. So he stood right next to her, wondering if she even realised she had his hand in a death-like grip, while the police asked if she could give a description of any of the attackers.

'I've seen some of them hanging around here before, but I've never caught them doing anything,' she said.

'Could you pick them out from mug shots?'

She shrugged. 'Maybe. Probably, some of them.'

'But not now,' Tom said firmly, having another go. 'Now she needs to go to hospital and get checked out. You can talk to her later.'

'I'll take her,' Ben said. 'You go back to Fliss and tell her Meg's all right. She'll be worried sick. I'll see you at the hospital.'

He put his arm round her, but she straightened up and gave him a defiant and only slightly wobbly smile. 'I'm fine, Ben. Just a bit sore here and there. I need to go and get showered and get into my uniform—'

'Don't be ridiculous!' he said flatly. 'There's no way you're going to work today. You're going to the hospital now, to get checked out, and once we're happy I'll bring you back here and you can get changed and…'

He ground to a halt. And what? And then he'd take her back to his place and look after her? The flat wasn't his. It wasn't even rented! There was no way he could take her there and play happy families! What on earth was he thinking about?

'I'll be fine, Ben. Stop fussing.' Pushing him aside, she limped over to what looked like a door onto the stairwell and let herself in with her keys.

He followed her, and she turned and gave him a tired smile.

'Ben, I'm all right, really. I'll get showered and

dressed, and I'll drive myself to the hospital as usual. I'll meet you there.'

'I'll wait,' he said, his voice implacable, and she shrugged and turned to the stairs.

'Suit yourself.'

He followed her all the way up to the fourth floor, pausing at the doorway.

'May I come in?'

She hesitated for a moment, then shrugged again. 'If you must. I warn you, it's untidy. Housework's never top of my to-do list somehow.'

His smile felt crooked. 'Nor mine. I promise not to run my finger over the furniture. Now, go and do what you have to do, and then we'll go and get you checked out.'

'I've told you, Ben, I can drive myself.'

'I don't think so. There's the small matter of your windscreen, for a start.'

'My…? The monsters!'

'Shoo,' he said gently, and pushed her towards the open bathroom door. 'I'll wait here.'

She wasn't long, and while he waited he wandered around her sitting room, picking up photos, books, scanning her CD collection scattered across the floor in front of her sound system—eclectic taste, he thought—and then he found a photo of her, abseiling.

Oh, hell, he thought, and then realised that after her attack she wouldn't be able to do it, and he felt a surge of relief. He'd forgotten all about it, but now he didn't have to worry. Well, not about that, anyway. He put the photo down and looked around, studying the slightly chaotic but nevertheless warm and friendly room that Meg called home.

His own flat in London was like a hotel room, cold

and unwelcoming and sterile. Safe, he thought, and was
busy telling himself that he didn't want to live like Meg
when she reappeared, looking pale but determined.

'Right. Let's go.'

He frowned at her uniform, but she stared back at
him defiantly and he gave up. He had no rights over
her—hell, he didn't want rights over her. This week had
dragged his emotions every which way to Sunday, and
absolutely the last thing he needed was to get involved
with Meg.

So he ushered her downstairs, dragged her away from
her furious cataloguing of the insults heaped on her car,
and took her to the hospital, where he handed her over
to Angie and gave Pete and the camera a quick run-
down of what had taken place.

Then she appeared looking a little miffed and gave
them a crooked grin.

'OK, guys, if you want to shadow me I'm on Triage,
so Rae may find she's got her work cut out. Sorry, Rae,
but Angie won't let me do anything more strenuous. I
just have to sit here in this little room and interview
people about their injuries and put them into categories.'

'Like grading apples,' Ben said with a grin.

'Just so. Think you can bear the tedium?'

He nodded. 'Absolutely. I think a nice quiet morning
is just what the doctor ordered. I'm with Angie on that
one.'

And so they were sitting there, Ben on the edge of
the desk beside her chair, Steve in the corner, Rae outside with Pete interviewing the patients as they arrived
and getting the OK, when a gang of youths straggled
in.

Beside him, Meg stiffened, and Ben picked up on it
instantly. 'Know them?' he murmured, and she nodded.

'I should do,' she said softly. 'They're the scallies who worked me over this morning. Let them come in. Steve, can you film them, please?'

And reaching for the phone, she called Security.

Her heart was pounding, but Ben was amazing. He strolled out into Reception, grinned at the boys and introduced himself, told them what the film crew were doing and stationed himself firmly between them and the door. And when Security turned up in the form of two burly young men in uniform, coinciding with the arrival of the police who'd arrived to interview her, the youths were trapped.

They tried to get away, arms swinging wildly, but the cocktail of drink and drugs they'd taken had left them utterly uncoordinated, and between the boys in blue and the film crew, they were squashed in seconds.

'I gather you know these lads,' the policeman said to Meg, busily trussing them up with nylon ties and lining them up on the seats in a mutinous row.

'We've met. Hello again, boys. Trashed any cars lately?'

'Are they definitely the ones?'

She nodded. 'Oh, yes. Without doubt.'

'Could you identify the one who hit you?'

She scanned them again and nodded at the ringleader.

'He's the one,' she said. 'He's probably got a bruise on his hand.' As he made a run for it Ben grabbed him by the scruff of the neck and stopped him in his tracks.

'I don't think so, sunshine,' he said, and was rewarded by him vomiting on the floor at his feet.

Meg leapt backwards out of range and tutted. 'I should make you clear that up,' she said, distaste in her voice. 'I don't like it when people do that—most particularly not when they've just trashed my car and beaten me up.'

She turned away, her stomach churning. 'I'll get them checked over and then you can take them away,' she said, and left Ben standing holding the ringleader at arm's length and looking as if he'd like nothing more than to punch his lights out.

Half an hour later the lads had been checked over and taken into police custody—the ringleader with a broken knuckle, courtesy of her car keys against her ribs—and her statement had been taken and the department restored to normal.

'Right. Back to Triage,' she said, and smiled at the waiting masses. 'Sorry about that, everybody. OK, who's next?'

CHAPTER SEVEN

'YOU must be out of your mind!'

'Why? I've got a bruised rib and a graze on my knee. I'll be fine by Saturday, Ben.'

His heart sank. There'd been a glimmer of hope...

'What if you find you're not, halfway down that building? I think you're being silly.'

'No, I'm not. It's important. We need a 3-D ultrasound for the hospital. It would be mainly for Maternity, but if we could have access to it for use in trauma cases and for diagnostic purposes it would be wonderful. And there are a whole lot of other charities if you don't like that one. Anyway, I don't see why you're so bothered about whether I do it or not. You can't bottle out anyway.'

'Oh, watch me,' he growled.

'Ben, you can't,' she said, her voice determined. 'There are so many people sponsoring you—and Pete will have a fit. It's just the sort of photo opportunity he loves.'

He sighed. Oh, well, determined or not, she couldn't make him do it. He'd just cough up a couple of hundred quid and that would be that, and Pete could go to hell. He wouldn't let a mere slip of a woman shame him into doing something so stupid.

Would he?

'I still don't think you'll be up to it,' he said, hanging on to the thread of hope like grim death, but she just laughed.

'You're so transparent,' she teased. 'Just because you don't want to do it.'

He didn't, but he was beginning to realise there was no choice. Like it or not, and he certainly didn't, this persistent little woman had got him committed. Still, there might be a trade-off.

'What are you doing on Saturday night?' he asked.

She blinked. 'Saturday night? What I usually do—watching telly.'

'No hot date?'

She laughed. 'Who with? No man in my life, and I've grown out of clubbing with the girls. The only hot date I'm likely to have is with a bubble bath.'

Just the thought was enough to send him into hyperdrive. 'I'll do you a deal,' he said, concentrating on the core business and summoning up his rapidly dwindling courage. 'I abseil down that blasted building with you, and you come to a function with me in the evening.'

Her eyes narrowed. 'A function?' she said suspiciously. 'What kind of a function?'

He sighed and scrubbed a hand round the back of his neck. 'The programme's been nominated for some stupid award. There's not a prayer of us winning it, but we have to dress up like penguins and go along and look suitably impressed.'

'You make it sound so appealing.' She chuckled, and then tipped her head on one side and looked searchingly at him as the penny dropped. 'Are we talking TV-style Oscars here?'

He nodded. 'Exactly,' he said wryly. 'And I really, really don't want to do it, but Pete's threatened me with death so I don't have a choice, and they'll all be there with their other halves.'

'So you need a partner for the evening—some decorative little bit of fluff to smile in all the right places and keep her mouth shut. Why me? There must be hundreds of beautiful women lining up to be seen in public with you—take one of them.'

'Hardly hundreds—well, not that I know about, anyway, and nobody I'd choose to spend the evening with. My notoriety seems to go to their heads. I want someone with me who can talk to me, not just use me as an excuse to pose for the cameras. I can't stand fluffy women with more looks than brains. I want someone ordinary—'

'So you thought of me,' she said wryly. 'Well, wow, cheers. At least I won't get the wrong idea—not after you've explained it so carefully.'

He sighed and dragged his hands over his face. Hell, this was going so horribly wrong. He tried again. 'That's not what I meant and you know it. You aren't going to be fazed by the media attention, the last thing you'll do is drool over me, and we could do it as part of the programme.'

'You mean it's work, so none of your regular girlfriends will get jealous?'

He sighed again. 'You really are determined to take this the wrong way, aren't you? There are no regular girlfriends—no any sort of girlfriends. There's no one in my life.' Not since…

She grinned, and he realised she was teasing. 'Ben, I'd love to come. I don't care why you're asking me, I can't think of anything more fun to do. The bubble bath just doesn't measure up. So, thank you for your gracious invitation. I accept. Especially as it means I have to dress up. And that means shopping. I wonder what Fliss is doing tonight?'

* * *

'He said what?'

'He wants someone ordinary.'

'And he thought of you?' Fliss hooted with laughter. 'Oh, poor, deluded man!'

Meg pulled a face and prodded the froth on the top of her coffee. 'He meant it. He really thinks I'm ordinary. He certainly doesn't fancy me. If he did he would have—' She broke off, but it was enough. Fliss was on it like a terrier on a rat.

'He would have what?' she asked, leaning forward, her eyes sharp with curiosity.

Meg sighed. 'Kissed me. On the beach. He was just that close…' She held her finger and thumb up, a fraction apart, and sighed again. 'I really thought…'

'Oh, dear,' Fliss said slowly. 'Oh, Meg. You really are in love with him.'

There was no point in denying it, so she nodded. 'I know. Stupid, isn't it? So you see, even though he thinks I'm ordinary, I still have to go, because it's all I'll get of him, and I can set the video recorder and stash the memory and live on it for the rest of my life…'

She broke off and fiddled with the froth, giving it much too much attention, until Fliss took the spoon firmly from her hand and set it down.

'Meg? Does he know how you feel?'

She shook her head. 'Of course not. And I still have no idea why he gave up medicine. Has Tom got any further with that?'

It was Fliss's turn to shake her head. 'No. You know men. They don't talk about stuff that matters. Apparently Ben moved away because Tom's first wife was coming on to him, but that's all they've talked about.

To be honest, they've both been too busy, and Ben tends to keep himself to himself.'

'I think he does rather too much of that,' Meg said pensively, then shook off her reflective mood. 'Come on, this won't get my dress bought, and I'm going to be on national television. It needs to be good.'

She pushed her coffee away and stood up. 'Where to first?'

'I got my dress.'

Ben frowned in puzzlement. 'Dress?'

'For the award ceremony? We are still going, aren't we?'

'Oh—that dress. Good. Yes, of course we're going.'

She tipped her head on one side and studied his face, but it was its usual unrevealing self. 'Having second thoughts?'

'About the abseiling? Try third and fourth. About the awards do? Absolutely not. Believe it or not, I want you to come. And I'm really sorry I put it so badly. When I said ordinary, what I meant was normal—and I'd be privileged to have you at my side.'

He sounded sincere enough, to her relief, because if he'd bottled out she'd have to take the dress back, and that would be a shame. Not nearly as much of a shame as not getting to spend the evening with him, though. She couldn't think about anything else, and the anticipation was killing her.

'Privileged, eh? You don't have to go that far!' He opened his mouth but she held up her hand to stop him. 'No. Don't say anything to spoil it. Privileged is fine, and I can even cope with normal. What time are we leaving?'

'Four?' he suggested. 'Kick-off is at seven, and we'll

need to change at the hotel when we get there—it's more convenient than my flat, and I haven't been there for ages, so goodness knows what it's like, and the company's booked rooms at the hotel anyway.'

Her heart hiccuped. Rooms, as in a room for each of the team to share with their partners, or a room each for her and Ben? It wasn't clear, and it wasn't a problem anyway, if they were only using them to dress in. Or were they? Perhaps she ought to know. 'Are we staying overnight?'

'I'd thought so. Is that a problem? I'll drive you back the following morning. You start late, don't you?'

She nodded her head. 'Yes. I'm working today, and tomorrow morning, then I've got tomorrow afternoon and Sunday morning off. I don't start till twelve.'

'And this fiasco you've dragged me into?'

She grinned. 'We're abseiling at one. We'll be finished by two, so that will be fine. We can leave after that.'

He pulled a face, so she smiled at him and patted his cheek. Mistake. The slight roughness of stubble went straight to her nerve endings—all of them—and left her tingling and aware. Stupid, stupid girl, she thought, and took a step back out of range of his aftershave.

Suddenly the prospect of spending not only the evening in Ben's company but possibly the night as well was doing crazy things to her heart. She ought to ask about the room, but for some reason she didn't want to. If he didn't mean them to be together and had got her a separate room, then so be it. And if by the end of the evening they did want to be together, she'd let fate take its course.

Dangerous, she warned herself. So, so dangerous. Sunday was the last day of filming, the last time they'd spend together. She'd be crazy to get any closer to him just before he disappeared out of her life for ever.

Insane.

Desperate.

'RTA coming in—two casualties, both male drivers. No other vehicles involved. Can we have you in Resus, Meg?'

She turned to Tom and nodded. 'Sure. Coming, boys?'

It was good and dramatic, Ben thought, watching Steve zero in on the gore and Pete go pale. A nice open fracture, with protruding bone and lots of groaning from the patient, and Meg doing her soothing hand on the fevered brow thing while she checked the drips, inserted another IV line and explained to the camera what was going on.

Tom worked in silence, apart from requests for tests, issuing instructions to the team and explaining things to the heavily sedated patient, and Ben had to admit it was a seamless exercise.

Behind them Nick Baker and Angie were working with another team on the other casualty, and the hum of activity punctuated by the beeps and hisses of the machines was exactly what the programme required.

Ben hated it, but because Meg seemed to realise how hard he found it, she was explaining everything without a prompt, and he didn't have to say a word until it was all over.

Then, because Pete would expect a debriefing and it was easier to give him what he wanted, Ben went through the injuries with Meg.

'He's got a fractured tibia—his shin-bone,' she explained. 'That was what you could see sticking through the skin, but the fibula, the little bone beside it, is also broken.'

'And when the orthopaedic registrar pulled it out straight—what was that for?' he asked, knowing the answer full well but going through the motions for the viewers.

'To restore the circulation to the foot as a matter of urgency, but it'll need surgery to realign the fragments and correct the deformity caused by the fracture. He's gone to Theatre now, but because the skin was broken they'll put on an external fixator, a sort of frame to hold it in place from the outside, a bit like scaffolding. It's better done that way from an infection point of view and it's the best way to locate all the fragments and pull them into line.'

'And how long will he be in hospital?'

She shrugged. 'A few days, maybe a week or two at the most. Probably less. You can mobilise fairly quickly with an external fixator, depending on the degree of trauma and the number of fragments and any other injuries.'

'Could we go up to the ward and meet him later?' Ben suggested, and she shrugged.

'I don't know. Possibly. Could be interesting to see it—and also Andy Johnson with his reattached hand. I'll find out for you. Maybe when I go off shift.'

She turned to Steve. 'Right, lose the camera. I'm on my break and I don't need watching while I eat breakfast! Ben? Are you coming?'

He fell in beside her, switching off both their mikes and following her down the corridor.

'Neatly done,' he said with a wry laugh. 'Where are we going?'

'One of the coffee-shops. There's a little one at the

back of the hospital which the staff seem to have taken over.' She shot him a thoughtful look. 'Are you OK?'

He didn't pretend to misunderstand. 'I'm fine. It's the machinery—the teamwork, the noises, the smells—all of it.'

'And it brings it back.'

He stopped in his tracks. 'Meg, back off,' he said flatly. 'I don't want to talk about it.'

'If you'd only tell me—'

'Well, I won't. Leave it—please, just leave it, or I'll...'

'What? Run away again?'

He met her eyes—kind, gentle eyes, thoughtful and caring. And curious. Not from idleness, but from a genuine need to know, to help him.

He felt the panic rising, the need to escape, to get the hell out.

And as if she realized that, she stopped pushing, just as he was about to turn and walk away. Her smile was apologetic.

'Sorry. Come on. We'll have coffee and a disgustingly sticky cake and go back and find something innocuous to do. Any suggestions?'

'Playing hookey again?'

She laughed. 'Look where that got us last time!'

He smiled ruefully. 'True. Any news of Jess?'

'She's out of danger, they think. She'll probably go home over the weekend. I spoke to the ward this morning. Apparently she wants to see us.'

'Without the camera,' he suggested hopefully, but Meg shook her head.

'She wants to be on the telly—awake and in her make-up.'

He sighed. 'Oh, well, it'll keep Pete happy,' he said, 'and if the producer's happy, he gets off my back. I'm all for that.'

They did go up to the wards later, and saw not only Jess, sitting up in bed and feeling much more alert and comfortable, but also Mick Jarvis, with his external fixator, and Andy Johnson.

Andy's wife and children were with him, and they seemed genuinely delighted that Ben had taken the trouble to go and see how he was getting on.

'I've got the circulation back to it,' he explained as Steve zoomed in on the lifeless limb lying supported on a pillow, 'and I can move it if I think hard, but that's only coming from the arm, not the hand, and there's no feeling in it. They've said that'll take ages,' he told Ben, and Ben nodded.

'Any pain?' he asked, and Meg's ears pricked up. Was this the anaesthetist in him sneaking out without him noticing, or the touchy-feely presenter getting down to brass tacks?

'A bit—more of an ache, and only in the arm, but I keep feeling things like cramp and itching in the hand when there isn't any. It's weird, but they tell me that's the nerve damage.'

Ben nodded again and lifted Andy's hand, as if he was going to examine the replanted limb, then suddenly seemed to realise what he was doing. He stuffed his hands in his pockets and stepped back. 'Well, good luck with it. I hope it mends well and you get back to work soon. Thank you for allowing us to film you.'

'You're welcome.'

'And don't come back,' Meg added with a grin. 'No more bits cut off. Can't you grow tomatoes under plastic?'

'I've told him that,' Jill said with a laugh. 'We're looking into it. Trouble is, all the glass would have to come down, and you know what that means!'

'Get a bulldozer,' Ben advised with a chuckle. Raising his hand, he waved farewell and they walked out of the ward, Steve panning after them.

'Great. Excellent. What now?' Pete asked.

'Now I'm going home,' Meg said. 'I need to pack for tomorrow and, frankly, I've had enough.'

'Can we film that?'

'No,' she said firmly. 'Nobody's interested in my flat or my clothes, and they sure as eggs aren't watching me in the bath!'

'But—'

'Pete, back off,' Ben said firmly, and took the mike from her. 'Enough's enough. Meg, we'll see you in the morning.'

She nodded. 'Don't forget to bring jeans and climbing boots, if you've got them, or trainers with flexible grippy soles.'

His jaw tensed. 'If you insist.'

'I do. I'll see you at seven.'

And before Pete could think of anything else he wanted to film, she walked briskly away down the corridor, ran down the stairs, grabbed her things from her locker and went out to the car park. Her windscreen had been replaced the day before, but the wiper was still broken and the aerial didn't work. Never mind. She'd get them fixed next week. It would be something to do when Ben had gone...

'Oh, hell,' she whispered, and stabbed the key into the ignition. She didn't want to think about Ben going, not at all, but he was going to, and there was nothing she could do to stop him.

*   *   *

Meg spent hours that night deep-conditioning her hair and doing her nails and packing for her trip to London. In fact, she was so wrapped up in the thought of Saturday night that it was only after she woke late the following morning and saw the abseiling crew setting up the ropes on the top of the surgical block as she drove in that she remembered.

Oh, hallelujah. Judgement day.

Damn. And, of course, she'd been so busy getting ready for tonight that she'd forgotten her clothes for the abseil. Great. She couldn't do it without her trainers, but then she remembered she'd lost them anyway on the beach. Unless…

She glanced down and saw her old pair abandoned in the footwell with a pair of her scruffiest jeans.

Blast. There was no getting out of it.

She nearly came to blows over the last parking place, but in the end the man trying to squeeze his car into the slot couldn't get out of the door and had to go elsewhere, and she shot neatly into the little gap, squirmed through the crack and made it into the department, trainers in hand, at a minute to seven.

'Ah, Spiderwoman,' Pete said.

She forced a smile at his weak joke and shot through to the staffroom, throwing her jeans and elderly trainers in her locker and washing her hands before checking in with the night sister.

'I'll be with you after hand-over,' she said to Steve as she paused in the doorway. 'I'm in charge today.'

'No, you're not, I've taken over,' Angie said from inside the room.

'But it's your day off! I was on the rota—'

'And you're too tied up with this lot and the abseil

to do it properly. It's fine. It's only a half day. Go on, I'll get my own back on you in due course.'

As if she was doing Meg a favour!

'No way,' she retorted with a grin. 'This is your fault, you landed me in it. Live with it.'

She shut the door and turned, to find Ben right behind her, his face unsmiling.

'So how much is it going to cost me to stay on terra firma?' he asked without preamble.

'And good morning to you, too. I have no idea. I have to make a few calls first, but I hope you're feeling rich, because at the last count it was over twenty-three thousand.'

His jaw sagged.

'How much?'

'Twenty-three thousand. I've got the local radio stations on it. Didn't I mention that? Obviously the listeners all love you.'

'Or hate me,' he growled. 'They'll probably all be lined up waiting for me to fall to my death—and, no, you didn't mention it.'

She cocked her head on one side, scanning his face a little more closely. His jaw was locked, the muscles jumping, and there was a little tic in his eye. 'You're truly worried about this, aren't you?' she said slowly.

'No, I'm just peachy,' he retorted sarcastically. 'I love the idea of hanging by a thread.'

'And there I thought it was just me,' she murmured with a grin. 'I tell you what—I'll hold your hand if you'll hold mine.'

'Or we could both run away.'

Tempting—and for more reasons than she cared to think about.

'Coward,' she said.

Behind her she heard him mutter, 'Dear God, you owe me.'

She wasn't quite sure who he was talking to, her or God, but one thing she was sure of. He was going off that building with her, come hell or high water.

'Get over it, Maguire,' she told him. 'You've got your pound of flesh. I'm coming with you tonight and not drooling and being normal and ordinary—remember?'

'Will you ever let me forget?'

'I might. Depends how nice you are to me.'

He snorted. 'I must have been mad. I could have got out of that, too, and now I'm doing both. I need my head examined.'

'Has that ever been in doubt? Whatever, we're doing this, both of us, so live with it. Right, what's going on this morning?'

By one o'clock the sponsorship total had climbed to over twenty-four thousand pounds. There was no way Ben had that kind of money sitting around. The bulk of his income went on living expenses, and anything that was left went to children's charities and the air ambulance service.

So there was no twenty-four thousand sitting in a savings account, waiting for him to give it away, because he'd already done it. Which meant only one thing.

Dammit.

'Got your stuff?'

He shot Meg a look that should have fried her skin, and hefted the bag in his hand.

'Right, let's get changed and go and register. I forgot to bring my stuff so I'm doing it in my grotty old jeans and ancient trainers that were lying on the car floor. I hope Steve hasn't got too strong a zoom on that camera.'

'We could always—' he began, but she just turned round, laughing, and dragged him into the staffroom.

'Change,' she ordered, so with a shrug he heeled off his shoes, yanked off his trousers and pulled on his jeans, trying not to look as she did the same.

Clearly she had no such inhibitions. 'Those jeans again?' she said when he was one leg in, one leg out. 'They're worse than mine,' she said, and he glared at her once more and dragged on the other leg.

'Don't you start. You're lucky I'm doing this at all, so don't push it.' He zipped them up, hitched the belt up an extra notch for security and put on his trainers.

'They need to be tight. You can't risk them falling all that way onto someone.'

'Would you stop it with the "all that way" stuff?' he growled, snapping to his feet, snatching up his trousers and shoes and stuffing them into the bag. 'Right, let's get this fiasco over with.'

Unfortunately it wasn't that easy. It took an age to register at the desk situated at the edge of the car park, and all the time Ben was conscious of a steady stream of lunatics pouring down the side of the building.

Madness. And some of them seemed to be having fun! He was given a harness, and someone clipped it on him and adjusted it to fit, tugging it good and tight. Great. It couldn't be tight enough as far as he was concerned. He fastened the helmet and felt the strap all but choke him.

'OK, we're on,' Meg said, and headed towards the doors. He turned and saw Steve grin and wave, and Pete was all but rubbing his hands together. Dammit. How on *earth* had he been talked into this?

He trailed Meg up in the lift and out onto the roof, and when she turned to say something to him he couldn't hear for the pounding of his heart. She frowned at him and reached out, her fingertips brushing the side of his neck.

'Your heart's racing!' she said. 'Are you OK?'

He closed his eyes briefly and sighed. 'No, Meg, I'm not OK. I don't do heights. I've been terrified of heights since I was three years old and got stuck on the ledge over the stairs. My mother had to get the fire brigade to rescue me, and I've never been able to cope with heights since. So, no, I'm not all right. I don't want to do this, but apparently we have to, so let's get it over with.'

She caught her lip in her teeth, her eyes full of remorse.

'You should have said—'

'I thought I had. Anyway, it's too late now. Let's just do it.'

Meg didn't think he was going to be able to make it, but he gritted his teeth, listened to the instructions and then, turning his back on the hellish drop, he leant back, walked down over the edge and paused for the obligatory photo.

'OK?' she asked, worried now and not happy with the responsibility, but stuck with it because yet again she'd known best and bullied someone into something against their better judgement.

She was always doing it, especially with something like this, but she'd never seen anyone so genuinely afraid as Ben.

'Just peachy,' he said, and, easing out his arm to give the rope some slack, he slid down a few inches.

'That's it. Bit more rope, a little bounce, and you'll drop down further.'

'Drop?' he said with a twisted grin, and she was relieved that he hadn't quite lost his sense of humour.

'Sorry.' She smiled back, her own fears forgotten in the process of helping him overcome his.

He tried again, going down a few feet this time, and she released her own rope and dropped down beside him. 'You're doing well. Keep going.'

'I intend to. I'm not spending the night here, tempting though it might be to miss the award ceremony. You wouldn't like to take my mind off it, would you?'

'How?'

'I don't know. Tell me about your underwear or something,' he suggested, his voice a little desperate.

He went down a few more feet, and she joined him and threw him a cheeky grin. 'What underwear?'

'The underwear you're wearing?'

'Like I said—what underwear?'

He turned his head and stared full into her eyes. 'No underwear?' he murmured.

'Well, I've got a bra on, but I thought I'd give the knickers a miss today...'

Another drop, another look.

'First you're sunbathing topless, now you're going commando. You're winding me up.'

'Am I? Only one way to find out.'

'You're on.'

And without another word, he let the rope out and dropped fifteen or more feet. She shot down after him, hardly able to keep up, and by the time they reached the bottom his eyes were glittering.

There was a massive cheer and flash bulbs were popping. There were girls begging for Ben's autograph, officials waiting for their harnesses and helmets, and he patiently shucked off the kit and signed the scraps of paper and shook hands and waved to the people who'd sponsored him.

Then taking Meg by the arm, with a smile plastered firmly on his face, he steered her round the side of the building and down an alley-way, then pushed her into a doorway, dragged her into his arms and kissed her.

Finally, she thought. Finally...

Finally!

Lord, she tasted good. Sweet and moist and firm, her tongue tangling with his, her pulse racing under his hand as his fingers closed around her breast and he groaned.

'Ben...'

'Shh.' His mouth found hers again, his hand sliding down, round into the small of her back and tunnelling down into her jeans to encounter...

Underwear. Soft, silky, slippery knickers, with little lacy panels on the hems, just where her firm, taut buttocks creased against her smooth, lean thighs.

He dragged her up against him, rocking his hips against her, desperate for the feel of her beneath him.

'You lied to me,' he moaned, and she gave a throaty, sexy chuckle.

'It got you down.'

'It got me up, is what it got me. I nearly fell off that building. All the blood diverted from my brain. Do you have any idea how dangerous that could have been?'

She laughed again, and he realised she was trembling, nearly as much as he was. Easing away from her, he kissed her softly then straightened.

'Later,' he vowed. 'We'll finish this later.'

If he lived that long.

CHAPTER EIGHT

THE hotel was humming, a hive of activity, people rushing here and there in preparation for the big night.

All the major TV companies were represented, and when Meg saw so many people she recognised hanging around the elegant foyer and greeting each other like old friends, it suddenly dawned on her just what she'd let herself in for.

'Ben, what on earth am I doing here?' she muttered, and he shot her a teasing grin.

'Being ordinary,' he reminded her, and she poked him in the ribs with a forefinger.

'Watch it.'

He chuckled and turned back to the desk as the uniformed receptionist greeted him with a friendly smile. 'Good evening, Mr Maguire. Welcome back—it's good to see you again. You're in room 38, third floor. Turn left out of the lift and it's on the right, overlooking the square. Is there anything you'd like sent up?'

He shook his head, then turned to Meg. 'Want anything?'

Only you.

'No, I'm fine,' she said.

'Could I ask you both to sign in?' the receptionist said, sliding a form towards them and studying Meg with discreet interest.

She wondered if Ben had ever brought a woman here before, and told herself not to be so stupid. Of course he had. Here, and all sorts of other places, no doubt.

It was obvious now that he'd expected them to share a room. Of course, the reservations had been made some time before, but she wondered if he'd even attempted to reserve a room for her since Thursday, when he'd suggested she should come, or if he'd always assumed that the woman who accompanied him would share his bed—whoever she might be?

Not that she'd done anything to dispel his illusions. The atmosphere in the car on the way down had been charged with sexual tension, and she'd known from that first kiss after their abseil exactly how the evening would end.

What she didn't know was what it would mean, if anything, for Ben.

And that troubled her. It made no difference to the outcome, but it made her wonder about her moral fibre. She'd never—ever—made love to a man she'd known for so short a time. And she'd never felt this way either, even after a lengthy relationship.

It made no difference that she knew it was only the one night, and that it might not mean nearly so much to Ben, because for her it was everything. The honeymoon, the swansong—all of it, hello and goodbye rolled into one.

It just would have been nice if he hadn't taken it quite so very much for granted.

He opened the door to their room and held it for her, and she went in, flicking on the lights, looking around curiously to see what the TV company would give him by way of accommodation.

The answer was, quite impressive. A spacious room, sumptuously furnished with a kingsize bed and a luxurious *en suite* bathroom, but it wasn't a suite of rooms, so there was nowhere apart from the bathroom for her to dress with any privacy. Crazy, really, but she just wanted somewhere she could get ready alone without him watching her. It probably hadn't even occurred to him.

Oh, rats. She simply wasn't sophisticated enough to deal with this famous and charismatic man who could have any woman he wanted, and probably did. She couldn't imagine any woman in her right mind turning him down, and anyone but her wouldn't hesitate to undress in front of him. On the contrary, they'd probably all jump at the chance!

And then, just when she was beginning to feel that it had all been the most hideous mistake, he astonished her by saying quietly, 'I tried to get another room for you but there wasn't one available, so this is your room. If I'm lucky, it'll end up being mine as well, but if not, I'll get a taxi to my flat. I just don't want you to think I'm taking you for granted, because I'm not. I'll need to change here, of course, but beyond that I'm expecting nothing from you, Meg. It's all down to you.'

Had he read her mind? The tension drained out of her, and she smiled at him with gratitude.

'It seems a very big bed for one person,' she said softly, and he searched her face for an endless moment before his mouth quirked into a crooked smile.

'I couldn't agree more.' Then he sucked in a deep breath and looked around. 'Um…you shower first,' he suggested. 'You'll probably need ages to do your hair and make-up afterwards, and we're running out of time.'

So she went and showered, the butterflies in her stomach not sure if they were excited or scared to death. The butterflies weren't alone, but she reminded herself she was a very small part of this event, little more than a table decoration, and the fear gave way to excitement and incredible, unbelievable anticipation.

Conscious of the time, she showered quickly and went out into the bedroom swathed in a soft, thick towelling robe she'd found on the back of the bathroom door, to find that Ben had vanished.

Or not. The curtains parted as he came back into the room, and she realised belatedly that they had a balcony. He had a glass in his hand, and he held it out to her.

'Here—Dutch courage. It's champagne. I reckon we've earned it.'

She eyed it dubiously, but then thought, what the heck. She'd had no lunch, and nothing much for breakfast. It would go straight to her head—which might give her the confidence to put on the dress.

'Thank you,' she said with a tentative smile, and his eyes darkened.

'Do you have any idea just how sexy you are, standing there like that, all pink and glowing and gorgeous?' he growled softly.

She laughed, but the laughter caught in her throat and she swallowed hard. 'Ben—'

'Shh. Later. I'll go and shower. Don't finish the bottle.'

'I won't.'

The bathroom door closed and she heard the lock slide to. She sipped a little more, then blotted her hair dry and flipped open her bag. If she dressed quickly, she would have that privacy she so perversely needed.

She hung up her dress, then rummaged in the bag for underwear. Such as it was. The only things she could wear under the dress were a strapless bra and the slightest, tiniest thong she'd ever seen, both a pale honey colour to disappear under the smoky lavender silk. At least they wouldn't show if there was a UV light on at any time!

Underwear on and with an illusion of security, she then dried her hair, thankful that for once it fell sleek and heavy to her shoulders without a kink. Amazing.

She puffed scent into the air and walked through it, then reached for the dress and slid it over her head. It slithered down heavily, rippling over her breasts and settling like a skin around her waist and hips. Cut on the cross, the hem fell from midcalf at the front to brush her heels at the back, and when she moved the silk parted to reveal a fleeting glimpse of leg.

Fortunately not the leg with the graze on it from her mugging the other day, or she wouldn't have bought it. Even now, she wasn't sure why she had. It was utterly unforgiving and she was amazed she could get away with it, but Fliss had assured her it was stunning, and anyway it was too late now to worry. At least she didn't have VPL with the tiny scrap of thong.

As a concession to the cameras and because she didn't want to let Ben down, she brushed a flick of muted shadow on her lids and a touch of tinted moisturiser with a hint of glitter over her cheeks. And lipstick, because even she wore lipstick from time to time.

But no mascara, because if Ben should win, she knew she would cry.

Straightening up, she slipped on her shoes and stood back to study herself in the mirror, and her eyes widened.

Was this her? This poised young woman with a slender waist and curving hips and—gracious, so much cleavage?

The nerves came back, just as the bathroom door

opened and Ben emerged in nothing more than a towel.
He stopped in his tracks, his hands pausing in the act
of knotting it at his waist, and his eyes met hers in the
mirror, then swept down over her body, cataloguing
every inch of it.

Then his eyes came back to hers, and he came slowly
up behind her and ran a finger over the bare expanse of
her shoulders, up, slipping it under the fine spaghetti
strap and running it round, down, to trail over the hollow between her breasts, his eyes never leaving hers in
the mirror.

'You're beautiful,' he whispered unsteadily. 'Quite
exquisite.'

'Not ordinary?'

His laugh cracked in the middle. 'Not in the least
ordinary,' he agreed. 'You never are, but this…' He
shook his head as if to clear it, and reached for his
clothes. 'If you don't want to be shocked you might
want to go on the balcony.'

'Maybe I want to be shocked,' she teased, suddenly
feeling the power of her womanhood, but he shook his
head again and pushed her gently towards the French
windows.

'Not that shocked. Go on. I don't want to scare you
to death.'

'You bragging?' she asked bravely, but she went anyway, the fortifying champagne in hand. She topped up
her glass from the bottle in the bucket outside and tried
not to think about Ben naked in the bedroom behind
her.

The balcony was lovely, overlooking the trees in the
square opposite and running the length of the room. She
breathed in the scent of the flowers that rioted in pots

clustered at each end and wished the evening was over and she was back here with Ben.

'Meg?'

She turned, to find him right behind her, an orchid in his hand.

He held it out to her, and she reached for it slowly. 'What is it?'

'It's for you. I thought…'

She smiled. He had. He'd thought—thought of her, gone to the trouble of arranging a corsage for her. Nobody had ever done that before, and she felt her eyes fill.

'Thank you, Ben,' she whispered, looking down as he held it against her breast. 'I felt undressed really, but I didn't have any jewellery that would do the occasion justice. I don't really do jewellery, but that's so beautiful.'

'I don't know where you think it ought to go. The dress doesn't need anything. Your hair?'

'Has it got a clip?'

He nodded, and she smiled. Flowers in her hair. How romantic.

'Do it for me,' she murmured, and he moved closer, the flowers giving way to the scent of his aftershave and the unique fragrance of his skin, all of it mixed into a heady potion that threatened to knock her off her feet.

Or was that the champagne?

'There,' he said, and stepped back, so that for the first time she got a good look at him, and her heart rate hitched up a gear.

He was wearing a tux, as she'd expected, but she'd never expected it to look so good on him. Beautifully cut from the finest, softest wool, the fabric draped over his body, subtly hinting at the sheer power of the muscular frame beneath. The sharpness of the black, in stark contrast to the brilliant white of the crisply pleated shirt, set off the natural warmth of his skin and emphasised the smouldering storm-grey of his eyes.

He took her breath away, and for a moment she was speechless. It was so unlike her that he tipped his head slightly to the side and frowned. 'What? Is my bow-tie crooked or something?'

She shook her head. 'No. I was just admiring you. You look gorgeous, Ben. Stunning.'

'Good. It'll keep the punters happy, and that means I get to eat.' He gave her a crooked grin and topped up his glass. 'To us,' he said softly, and her heart nearly stopped.

He was talking as if they might have a future, as if there was more to this night than just these few short hours.

No. Don't be silly. She smiled. 'To us,' she echoed.

'The nominations for best fly-on-the-wall documentary are as follows: *Under the Arches*; *Unsung Heroes—the Fire-fighters*; and *Revealing All*.'

There was a shuffle and a ripple of conversation, as people turned to look at the nominees, and then clips of each of the programmes were shown on a huge screen above the podium. *Under the Arches* was about homeless kids in London, with a deeply evocative and simple clip that nearly reduced Meg to tears, and *Revealing All* was a look into the lives of young prostitutes in Manchester. The clip from Ben's programme showed him coming out of a blazing building dragging a fire-fighter to safety, and seeing it again made Meg's throat close with fear for him. It somehow seemed so much more real now that she knew him.

'And the winner is…' There was a pause while the Master of Ceremonies slit open the envelope with a flourish and pulled out the card, '*Unsung Heroes!*'

There was a massive round of applause, and Ben shook his head. 'Crazy,' he muttered, and he and Pete Harrison got to their feet and went up onto the platform to receive their award, taking Steve with them—about the only time Meg had seen him without a camera in hand. Her palms hurt from clapping, and her eyes were filling, as she'd known they would, but Ben was talking now, thanking everyone, and most particularly the personnel at the fire station who had made it possible.

'The men of the Green Watch were fantastic. They treated me as one of their own, part of the team, and gave me an insight into the danger that they face every day of their lives. I'll never take a fire-fighter for granted again. It was a privilege to work with them, and I'd like to thank them for giving me that opportunity, and for making the filming of the programme possible.'

They turned to leave the platform, but the MC reached out a hand and held Ben back.

'There is just one more thing. I understand the chief fire officer gave you a commendation for bravery, but you declined it.'

Ben's face froze. 'I did—because I didn't do anything to deserve it. How did you find out about it?'

'We were approached, when the nominations were announced. You see, there's someone who disagrees with you, and he's here tonight. You've all seen him already once this evening, on the clip. He's the man Ben dragged out of a blazing building, and I'd like to introduce him to you now. Ladies and gentlemen, Station Officer Sam Peck!'

Ben straightened and turned, his face a mass of emotions as a man came through an opening at the back of the platform and took him by the hand.

'Sam, what's going on?' Ben muttered, but Sam gave a grim smile and turned to the spellbound audience.

'On the 28th of April last year, I was inspecting the premises you've just seen after my crews had been called to a fire there. It had been burning for some considerable time, and we thought it was contained. I went in with Ben to inspect the damage and to check that there were no hot spots, but when I opened one of the office doors, I experienced the fire-fighter's nightmare—a backdraught. I let oxygen into the room by opening that door, and it fed the flames and created a fire-ball that blew me off my feet. It was only Ben's prompt and courageous action in dragging me away from that inferno that saved my life.'

He turned to Ben, his face utterly serious. 'Ben, you reckon you don't deserve this commendation, but I happen to know you're wrong, because without you, I would have died in that fire, and left a widow and three small children. So, I'm sorry, it's tough, but you're having it—from me, and from my wife and kids, and from all the men of Green Watch—and if you ever want a job, you've got one at my station.'

The room erupted. Sam picked up the award from the rostrum and handed it to Ben, then shook his hand again.

Ben shook his head wordlessly, then dragged Sam into a hug that should have crushed him. Then he let him go and turned and made his way back to the table, his face twisted with emotion.

The applause was still thunderous, and Meg didn't care that the cameras were on them and tears were streaming down her face, because she was so proud of him she could have burst...

The door closed behind her with a quiet click, and Ben crossed the room and put the awards down on the table, his face expressionless.

'Thank God that's over,' he said with a heartfelt sigh, and stripped off his bow-tie and draped his jacket over the back of a chair. 'I thought the party was never going to end. I wonder if the champagne's still worth drinking.'

He opened the balcony door and went out, drawing in a deep breath and closing his eyes. He looked exhausted, and Meg refilled their glasses with the remains of the champagne and handed him one.

'Congratulations,' she said softly. 'I'm really proud of you.'

'Don't.'

'But I am.'

She smiled and stepped closer, cradling his jaw in her hand, and he turned his head and pressed a soft, lingering kiss to her palm.

'You look beautiful,' he murmured. Lifting his hand, he unclipped the flower from her hair and set it down, then, putting the glass down, he drew her into his arms, threaded his fingers through her hair and lowered his mouth to hers.

'I've been longing to do this all night,' he murmured, brushing his lips against hers. Then he slanted his mouth over hers and claimed her with a kiss so hot, so needy, so hungry that her legs nearly buckled.

Then he eased away, rested his forehead against hers and sighed gently. 'I must be insane. Only a fool would expect to get up before six, put in five hours' filming, abseil down an absurdly high building—how high was it?'

'Nine storeys. Did I tell you how proud I was of you for doing that?'

'No, you didn't. I hope Steve got plenty of footage, because I'm never—ever—doing it again. Dear God. Where was I? Oh, yes. Abseil down a nine-storey building, then drive to London, put on fancy togs and go to a highly public dinner followed by some crazy award ceremony screened live on national television, party half the night and then take a woman he really, really wants to impress to bed and expect to do her justice.'

Meg laughed softly and wrapped her arms around his waist, hugging him closer and looking up into his eyes, unbelievably touched by his honesty.

'You don't need to impress me, Ben. You don't need to do anything. You can go to sleep if you want. Just hold me.'

His brows drew together and he swallowed hard. 'Don't worry, I intend to,' he said gruffly. Placing his hands on her shoulders, he turned her and steered her back into the bedroom.

He closed the balcony door, dimmed the lights and then drew her back into his arms. For a moment all he did was hold her, then he lowered his head and nuzzled against her hair. His lips found her ear, her throat, the little hollow at the base where her pulse was racing. He soothed it with his tongue, then moved on, downwards, leaving a trail of fire over the soft swell of her breasts, down to the endless cleavage she'd been so conscious of all evening.

'You feel so good—so soft,' he murmured, and his hands slid round her ribs and cupped her breasts, lifting them to his mouth. With a groan he lifted his head and searched her face with his glittering eyes.

'We have too much on,' he said roughly, and he stared at the dress in frustration. 'How does this come off?'

Oh, Lord. What if the sight of her naked turned him off? But he didn't look as if it would. In fact, he looked as if he'd die of frustration if she didn't do something soon. She swallowed the little surge of panic and stepped back a little, slipped the straps down over her arms and slowly, carefully, wriggled out of it, letting it fall in a shimmering pool at her feet.

His eyes followed its path, then jerked back up again, fixing on her chest.

'Dear God—Meg!' he whispered, his face horrified, and for a moment all her fears about her body came to life. Then his hand reached out, his fingers outlining the livid bruise on her ribcage where she'd been punched, and she breathed again.

'It's OK. It looks much worse than it is.'

He shook his head and swallowed. 'Bastards,' he growled softly, then looked up at her and met her eyes. 'Are you really OK?'

'I'm fine—or I would be if you'd stop torturing me with this endless waiting.'

His eyes darkened and, without taking them off her, he unbuttoned his shirt with unbearable deliberation, removed his cuff-links and shrugged the shirt off his shoulders. His hands, free again, moved to the trousers, those beautifully cut, soft wool trousers that did nothing to hide his feelings from her.

He heeled off his shoes, hooked his thumbs in the waistband of his trousers and boxers and stripped them off, picking up his socks *en route* so that when he straightened he was gloriously, magnificently naked.

He took her breath away. He was—oh, God, so very, very aroused, and for a moment she felt a flicker of panic, but her body had no such hesitation and she felt the sharp pull of desire deep within her. She needed him—needed him as she'd never needed anyone or anything, and if he didn't hold her soon, she was going to die.

He dropped the trousers in a crumpled heap on top of the shirt, and she thought, totally inconsequentially, They'll crease.

And then he reached out a hand to her, and she took it and stepped out of her dress and into his arms, the trousers forgotten.

His hands slid down her back and cupped her bare bottom, and a groan erupted from deep in his throat. 'These are *not* knickers,' he said unsteadily, his fingers tracing the thin silky band back up to her waist and round, skimming the trembling plane of her abdomen, then up, over her quivering midriff to the centre clasp of her bra.

It fell open at his touch, and with a ragged sigh he eased it away from her and shook his head.

'You lied—about the topless sunbathing,' he said flatly, and she gave a shaky little laugh.

'I didn't lie. I believe I was noncommittal, and told you you didn't need to get to know me that well.'

'I was jealous,' he confessed, his eyes caressing her. 'I'd never even met you before, but the thought of another man seeing you...'

He lifted his hand and grazed his knuckles over the aching, swollen curve of her breasts, along the edge of her tan line, and she closed her eyes and whimpered with need.

'Please—Ben—touch me,' she whispered, and then she felt the heat of his mouth on her skin and her knees buckled.

He caught her, hauling her against him, his restraint finally shattering as his frenzied mouth found hers and plundered it. Her hands raided his back, searching out the corded muscles, the hollow of his spine, the firm, taut swell of his buttocks. Moaning against his mouth, she pulled him closer, rocking against the hot, heavy steel of his erection and dragging another groan from deep inside him.

'I need you,' he rasped. 'Dear God, Meg, I need you now...'

His mouth ravaged hers again, and then with a gasp he wrenched himself away.

'Ben?'

'Condoms,' he muttered. 'Where the hell's my jacket?'

'On the chair,' she said, hysterical laughter bubbling in her throat.

'Damn. Wrong pocket.'

He came back to her, his hands brimming, and her jaw sagged. He smiled grimly. 'I ransacked the machine in the gents,' he told her, and she laughed again.

'I hope nobody else thought they were going to do this tonight,' she said, and he laughed and pulled her back into his arms.

'You are so lovely,' he said, and the laughter left them, replaced by a tender urgency. 'I want to make love to you.'

'I thought you were.'

'I haven't even started yet.'

Her heart nearly stopped. She found a smile from somewhere and cradled his dear, beloved face in her hands. 'Don't let me stop you,' she murmured, and drew him down for her kiss.

'I'm starving.'

Ben laughed and propped himself up on one elbow. He felt happy and relaxed and more in tune with himself than he'd felt in years, and Meg was single-handedly responsible.

'Starving, eh?'

'Mmm. I hardly ate a thing last night—too many nerves.'

'You were nervous?' he said, and chuckled. 'I thought it was me who had to be nervous.'

'I was doing it for both of us,' she said ruefully, propping herself up on both elbows and reaching her face up to kiss him. 'Mmm.' She rubbed her chin gently against his, and wrinkled her nose. 'Stubble,' she murmured.

'I'll shave.'

'No. No, don't. I like it.'

'It'll make your face sore.'

'Depends how much you intend to kiss me,' she said with a smile, and he slid his free hand round the back of her neck and anchored her.

'A lot,' he mumbled against her lips.

They came up for air a minute later, and she pushed him away. 'OK, I agree. You need to shave. But breakfast first.'

'It's only five-thirty.'

'Habit. I always wake up at five-thirty.'

He pushed back the quilt and looked down at her, scanning the soft, full breasts, the slender waist, the slight hollow of her pelvis above the dark curls. His hand ran down, palm flat against her skin, and curled around her hip, rocking her against him so she could feel what she did to him.

Her eyes widened and she smiled. 'Well, good morning,' she said softly.

'Good morning.'

He lowered his head and kissed her again, but after a moment she pushed him away. 'Uh-uh. You haven't shaved, and I still need breakfast.'

He gave up. With a frustrated laugh he swung his legs over the edge of the bed and picked up the phone. 'What do you want?'

'Something exotic. Actually, I could murder a huge cup of tea.'

'Something exotic. Right. So I'll ask for tea, shall I?' he teased, and she laughed and hit him with a pillow.

'Pig. Tea and…'

'Mmm?'

'Toast. Hot buttered toast, and honey—Greek yoghurt and runny honey, and…' she paused thoughtfully. 'Grapes.'

He placed the rather strange order, added scrambled eggs and smoked salmon just for good measure and took himself off to the bathroom for a quick shower and a shave, before he flayed her skin off while he kissed every inch of it all over again.

'Room service!'

He dragged the robe on and opened the door, tipped the waiter and set the tray down on the end of the bed, moving the tea to the relative safety of the table before climbing back into bed with her and feeding her.

Perversely she decided she fancied the scrambled egg and smoked salmon, so they shared it, then the yoghurt and honey, and then he fed her grapes while she lay sprawled against the pillows, sipping tea and sighing in contentment.

'Better,' she said, and handed him the cup. 'More?' she asked, and he topped up her cup and handed it back, happy just to watch her. She truly was lovely, with her amazing eyes that went from azure to midnight when he kissed her, and that gorgeous, voluptuous body that welcomed him so beautifully.

Just now she was looking at him with those blue, blue eyes and smiling enigmatically. 'So tell me,' she said. 'Do you make love to all the people you shadow?'

Ben's mouth twitched. 'Only the women,' he replied, and she rolled her eyes and threw a pillow at him. He fielded it with a smile, then looked back at her, his smile fading. Suddenly he didn't want to tease her. Not about this. It was too important. 'I've never done it before,' he said quietly.

'What, not even with the war correspondent? She was pretty.'

'Lena Murray? She wasn't my type.'

'And I am?' she said in disbelief.

'Oddly, yes,' he told her with a slow smile, 'otherwise I wouldn't be here.'

Her answering smile was contented. 'Good,' she murmured. Putting the cup down, she slid out of bed looking curiously self-satisfied, and disappeared into the bathroom.

So she was his type. Good, she thought as she showered, because he was certainly hers. If only he would open up to her, but she was getting there, surely? And before he left to return to London, with any luck, they would have discussed seeing each other again.

Meg pulled a face. Long-distance relationships seldom worked, but she'd give this one her best shot. She went back into the bedroom five minutes later, her bare skin still damp from her shower, and dropped her towel on the floor. 'Now. About this shave you've had. It would be a shame to waste it,' she murmured, and reached for him with a smile.

He lifted his hand to her, and she took it and climbed onto the bed, then as she knelt down beside him, she caught sight of the look on his face and had another moment of insecurity.

'What is it?'

His fingers touched her, running over her ribs, tracing the bruise with infinite care.

'How dare they?' he said unsteadily, and looked up into her eyes. 'I could kill them.'

She felt the tension leave her. 'They're just kids. They were panicked.'

'They'd better stay away from me or I'll give them something to panic about,' he growled, and, sitting up, he bent his head and laid his lips tenderly, reverently, on the purpled skin.

'Ben?'

'Mmm.'

'Make love to me,' she whispered, and he lifted his head and met her eyes, his own stormy with desire.

'I intend to,' he murmured. Drawing her gently into his arms, he cherished every inch of her, until her heart felt as if it would burst with emotion and her body was screaming for release.

Then he moved over her, filling her, body and soul, and she fell headlong into paradise.

CHAPTER NINE

'Last day of filming.'

'Mmm. Maybe my last ever,' Ben said, his voice thoughtful.

Meg swivelled round in the car seat and stared at him in confusion.

'Really? Pete's talking about the next series.'

'I know. And I've suddenly realised I've had enough. Enough drama, enough publicity, enough of him nagging at me and giving me hell and then taking all the credit.'

She could understand that. Watching them together, she was amazed their relationship had lasted as long as it had.

'So what will you do next?' she asked, watching him carefully.

His shrug was so slight she hardly saw it. 'I have no idea. Drive lorries?'

'Do you have your HGV licence?' she asked, realising she wouldn't be surprised if he said yes, but he shook his head.

'No. I don't know, I might take Sam Peck up on his offer.'

Meg felt her brows pleat together. 'But—that's crazy! Ben, you're a doctor. All that training and talent going to waste.'

'Hardly a waste, if I do something vital and useful like fire-fighting.'

But her heart was pounding, and she saw the clip

again in her mind, the flames following them out of the doorway, and wondered what on earth was driving him.

'Do you have a death wish?' she asked bluntly, but he just laughed, a short, humourless laugh that spoke volumes.

'Not really.'

'Then—why?'

'Because I have to earn a living, and I don't want to do the only thing I'm trained to do.'

She opened her mouth, but he saw out of the corner of his eye and shook his head slowly.

'Don't go there, Meg. Please.'

So she said nothing, although her mind was churning and her heart was pounding and she just wanted to make him stop and talk to her, tell her, finally, at last, just exactly what it was—

'It's nearly twelve. We'd better go straight there. Have you got a uniform at the hospital?'

She nodded. 'Yes—I've got the stuff I took off yesterday. It may be a little crumpled, but I can always wear scrubs. What about you?'

He glanced down at himself and pulled a face. 'Not ideal, but it'll do. I tend to wear the same thing so we can cut from one scene to another without the time thing being so obvious, but it's probably better to be there, and at least it's not my favourite jeans.'

She gave a little chuckle and rolled her head against the headrest, watching him as he drove. 'Why do you wear them?'

'Because it annoys Pete,' he said frankly, and shot her a cheeky grin. 'Do I need another reason?'

The place was heaving. The car park was always crowded on a Sunday, because of people visiting their sick relatives, but it was even busier than usual, and when they walked into A and E they saw the reason.

It was packed, and the receptionist gave Ben a pointed look in warning.

'Uh-oh. Your fame has obviously spread,' Meg murmured, and hustled him through the doors to the clinical area before the entire population of the waiting room could leap up and follow them.

Not that he needed much hustling. He'd taken one look at the crowd, composed mainly of women, and his heart had sunk. It was due to the television coverage of the abseiling yesterday, of course, with the local TV news crews there in force, and there was no way Pete would have wasted such a God-given opportunity. And then, just to add insult to injury, the award ceremony had been on television as well.

Damn.

'Oh, it's Mr Popularity,' Angie said, appearing from Resus and grinning at them. 'If I give you a white coat, would you like to deal with them? They seem to be here for you.'

His heart thudded against his ribs. 'Please, don't bother,' he said mildly, dredging up a smile and looking around. 'Where are Steve and Pete and Rae?'

'Here somewhere. Pete was fretting.'

'I don't doubt it,' he muttered, so that only Meg could hear, and he gave her a strained smile. 'You'd better change, and we'll see if we can get through the day without too much grief. At least Rae won't have to struggle to get consent. On second thoughts, I'll go and find whoever's on Triage and pay them to send everyone home.'

Meg laughed and headed for the staffroom. 'See you

in a minute,' she said, and he nodded and watched her go, his heart unaccountably aching.

Their last day together.

The thought was curiously unpalatable. Maybe they could see each other—carry on a relationship from wherever he ended up?

Wherever that might be. As sure as hell it wouldn't be a hospital. He could hear the hiss of a ventilator as the door to Resus opened behind him, and the bleeps and urgent commands and the smell of blood assailed his senses and brought bile to his throat.

He was about to bolt when Meg reappeared, dressed in clean scrubs and with her hair caught back in a ponytail. As she walked briskly towards him, the others in tow, he noticed her lip. His finger touched it lightly, his brow creasing in consternation.

'I've given you whisker-burn,' he murmured, and she smiled ruefully.

'It has been noticed,' she said, and he flicked a glance over her head to Pete, watching him with a mocking half smile on his face.

He wanted to flatten him and, as if she'd read his mind, Meg laughed and shook her head.

'Not him—Rae. She's lent me her make-up. I'm going to touch it up. I won't be long.'

She disappeared again, and Ben took the initiative. 'Well, you've done a good job at pulling in the crowd,' he said to Pete, the sarcasm in his voice thinly veiled. Pete just sighed heavily and ran a hand through his hair.

'What does it take to satisfy you? They pay your salary. Either you want this show to be a success or you don't. So you're popular. It got you an award—two, in fact—so don't whinge.'

'One of the awards had nothing to do with me being

popular,' he pointed out bluntly. 'And I didn't want either of them, so don't bother to hold them over my head. And for what it's worth, I've had it with your damned show, so make the best of today. It's my last.'

'All set!'

He turned towards Meg's voice with relief, and ignored Pete's furious explosion behind him. 'Right. Let's go.'

'What's eating him?' she asked as they walked towards the waiting room.

'I just told him I'm leaving,' he said. 'I don't expect him to take it lying down. The first thing he'll do is tell me to pull myself together, then he'll offer me more money. Then he'll threaten me with legal action, and finally he'll let me go, because he has no choice. It won't be pretty, but frankly I don't give a damn.'

'Well, it's certainly going to be an interesting afternoon,' she said with a grin, and opened the door to the waiting room.

It was hellish.

OK, the waiting room had more than its fair share of malingerers, but there were still plenty of people in need of medical attention, and Meg spent the next four hours stitching and swabbing and strapping, while Pete stewed quietly in the background and prayed for drama.

Ben was wonderful. He entertained the children, charmed the women and sympathised with the men. The whole lot of them were eating out of his hand by the end of it, and just about all of them had seen the abseil or the awards on television the night before.

And then, finally, Pete's prayers were answered. In spades.

'Meg, I need you,' Tom said, sticking his head round

the cubicle curtain. 'Sophie can finish up here—we've got a call-out to an RTA. They want a team and you're the only free senior nurse.'

She nodded, apologised to the patient for leaving her in the lurch, filled Sophie in and then went quickly to the staffroom. She pulled on green overalls that said NURSE on the back in yellow letters, grabbed the bag of kit from stores and ran after Tom, with Ben and Steve in tow, and Pete and Rae bringing up the rear.

'Ben, Steve, you come with us in my car—you two follow,' Tom told them, and it was only as she climbed into the front of the car and turned to talk to Ben in the back seat that she got a good look at his face.

She could see the muscles bunching in his jaw, his throat working, the pulse in his neck leaping in time to his racing heart. She'd seen him like this yesterday, just before they'd abseiled down the surgical block, but now there was no trace of humour and as Tom recounted the information he'd been given, the tension in his face seemed to mount.

'Five adults, two children in two cars. There's at least one fatality, and three entrapments. It won't be pretty, I'm afraid.'

Ben's jaw clenched and unclenched. It was obvious this was the last place on earth he wanted to be, but there was nothing she could do about it. Tom put the siren on and they sliced through the traffic and arrived at the crash scene within five minutes. Forgetting about Ben, she ran with Tom to Mike, the paramedic, who brought them up to speed.

'Three adults in the taxi here. The driver's dead, the others are still in the back but seem all right for now. The fire brigade are here, they'll unjam the doors to let them out when they've finished with the other car, but it's in much worse shape. Kenna's there, holding the driver's head still till we can get a rigid collar on. Head, neck and internal injuries, I reckon, and possibly lower limb. She'll fill you in. Female front seat passenger was unconscious when we arrived, but she's come round now and is in pain—trapped by the legs—and one of the kiddies in the back's looking bad. We can't get to him, though, till they've finished with the cutting gear, and Mum's fretting.'

'I'll start there, Meg, you triage these for me,' Tom said, and Meg quickly checked the three in the first car, then ran over to Tom.

'Right, they're both stable and relatively unharmed. Couple of fractures and contusions, but nothing major obvious. They're crying and talking, and Mike's with them. They'll be OK for a while, but there's not a mark on the driver. I think he might have died at the wheel. What about you?'

'We need to get them out,' Tom said quietly, straightening up so the woman couldn't hear him. 'I think the driver's in a bad way—possible cardiac tamponade—and his feet seem to be trapped, so we can't get him out. The woman's trapped and drifting in and out of consciousness, and she's very scared for the kids and her husband. See if you can find out what's going on in the back. I can't see the kids, but I can hear crying—sounds like one only, though.'

'That's the little one,' Kenna said from her position at the driver's head. 'I can just see him.' She lowered her voice. 'The older one's looking rough, Mr Whittaker. He's struggling for breath. You need to get in there.'

But because the car was buried in the hedge they couldn't, not until the fire brigade had finished lifting the roof clear an endless minute later, then Meg got her first proper look at the occupants and her heart sank.

The children in the back were only small, and the woman was moaning fretfully, her face covered in blood from an oozing head wound. 'Tom, she's pregnant,' she said, and behind her she heard Ben's indrawn breath.

'Dear God, I can't do this,' he said softly, and she turned in time to see him bending over the ditch, retching helplessly.

She would have gone to him, but the children needed her, and she crawled over the wreckage, pausing to press a hand on the woman's shoulder in reassurance, and took a tiny, frightened hand in hers and spoke gently.

'It's all right,' she said, talking to all of them, 'you'll be OK. Don't be scared.' The little fingers tightened, and she realised the hand was in a cast.

A blue cast, with a picture of a train on it.

'Adam?' she said, and the little head turned towards her and he sobbed in terror. Oh, dear Lord.

'Adam, it's Meg—remember me? It's all right,' she said again. 'We'll get you out in a minute.' Her free hand found Mrs Bright's shoulder, squeezing it again. Fingers came up and wrapped around hers and hung on for dear life while Meg ran her eyes worriedly over the other child. His chest was heaving, but the breath sounds were laboured and deteriorating as she watched. 'Tom, how are you doing?'

'Not good. The driver's definitely got a cardiac tamponade. I'm going to have to draw the blood off if we're going to save him. How are the kids?'

'The oldest has severe breathing difficulties. We have to get him out fast. The youngster's Adam—Adam

Bright. We've been treating him for a fractured radius. He seems OK. He's moving freely and there's no obvious sign of injury, but doesn't need to be in here.'

As she spoke her hands were running over him, checking his little body rapidly. Finally satisfied that he was safe to move, she unclipped his straps and lifted him clear of the car seat.

'I'll take him.'

She looked up, stunned to see Ben there holding out his hands, and she put the little lad into them without hesitation. He lifted him clear and cradled Adam against his chest, shielding him from the horrors all around, and she turned her attention to the other boy.

'Tom, he's getting worse. Someone needs to check Mrs Bright, but I've got my hands full.'

'So have I. I'm trying to insert a needle into this guy's chest in less than ideal conditions, and I need your help. Tell me about him. What's going on?'

'He's got a throat injury, I think—there's a toy tucked into the seat belt. It doesn't seem to have penetrated...' She checked again, and nodded. 'But his throat's swelling and his resps are way up. He needs intubating now to protect his airway, or he's going to need a laryngotomy.'

'I can't leave this man, Meg. We need back-up.'

'No time. I'll start ventilation for now. Get me oxygen and a bag-valve mask! And somebody call another team, please! We need an anaesthetist here *now*!'

She met Tom's eyes over the back of the driver's seat, and they both froze.

'We've got one,' Tom said grimly, and looked up. 'Ben.'

'Don't ask me,' Ben said, standing by the car with Adam cradled in his arms, the little head burrowed firmly into his neck, hiding from the horror while Ben's hand stroked his back, up, down, up, down…

'I'm not asking you, I'm telling you,' Tom said, his voice hard. 'I don't know what your problem is, Ben, but if you don't intubate that boy he could die! If you can stand there and let that happen, then you aren't the man I thought you were.'

'Please—save him,' Mrs Bright said brokenly, and Ben's face contorted. For an endless moment he stood there, his face racked with emotion, then he thrust Adam into someone's arms and climbed over into the back seat.

'Let me see,' he said, moving Meg aside, and his hands swiftly, thoroughly checked the child. 'Damn, he's very cyanosed. Meg, give him 100 per cent oxygen while I set up. Somebody show me where the kit is! He'll need anaesthetising and intubation.'

Behind Meg there was a flurry of activity, but she didn't look. She couldn't. She was too busy holding the mask over the boy's face, squeezing oxygen into him from the cylinder feeding it, the steady rhythmic hiss of the bag drowned out by the sound of the cutting gear racing to free the parents in the front.

Mike was checking Mrs Bright now, calming her, telling her the baby was fine, reassuring her while Meg struggled with the seal on the mask and tried to stop the other child from dying.

'OK. Let's do this. He needs more oxygen first. Keep going while I anaesthetise him. He's too light at the moment, he'll fight me. Can someone apply cricoid pressure, please?'

Meg did it, using her thumb while her fingers held the mask, stopping any possibility of reflux from the stomach into the airway until it was secured.

Ben found the vein with the first try, secured the cannula and injected the anaesthetic, the first part to knock the child right out, the second part to paralyse him so he could be intubated without distress. As the muscle relaxant took effect, Meg felt him twitch, and immediately, without moving his neck but simply lifting his jaw forward, Ben slipped the laryngoscope into his mouth and then slid the tube in while Meg continued to press down on the cricoid ring to bring his vocal cords into view.

'OK, cricoid off,' he snapped, rapidly attaching the tube to the bag valve and oxygen supply. It had taken mere seconds, and immediately the child started to pink up again.

'Stethoscope,' he said, and someone put one in his hand. He checked the boy's lungs for breath sounds as he bagged him, and then nodded.

'OK. We're in. We need to get him out of here. He's trapped by the seat. Can someone shift it fast? I want him out of here now!'

The woman had already been removed from the car the moment her spine had been secured, and the seat was freed and hauled out of the way, releasing the child's feet.

The operation to remove him from the car took moments once his spinal board was in place, and then he was away, into the ambulance and rushed to hospital, with Ben still working on him.

Meg watched them go, then turned back to Tom.

'OK. What now?'

'He's OK. I've done it—got about thirty mils out and he's looking better. Well done, Meg, you did a good job on the boy. Right, can we get this man out of here, please? What about the other car?'

'They're out,' she told him. 'They've gone already.'
He nodded.

'Right. You need to get back to Ben. Take my car,
I'll follow in the ambulance with Mr Bright. What about
the little one?'

'He's gone. He went with his mother.'

'Then go and find Ben.'

Easier said than done. By the time she arrived at the
hospital, they told her he'd left.

'Angie, I have to go to him.'

Angie, full of wisdom and human compassion,
needed no explanation. She'd seen this coming for days,
and she gave Meg a gentle push towards the door. 'Go
on. We'll manage.'

'The film crew...'

'Leave them to me. I'll keep them away.'

'Thanks.'

She fled, taking Tom's car because hers was still at
her flat where she'd left it yesterday, and drove to the
Red House. His car was there, and without knocking or
ringing the bell she went in and ran up the back stairs
to his flat.

'Ben?'

'Not now.'

He was dressed only in a towel, his skin reddened
from the shower. She guessed he'd been scrubbing it,
scrubbing off the blood—and the memories?

She followed him into the bedroom and wrapped her
arms around him from behind. 'Talk to me.'

'I can't.'

'Please...'

'Meg...'

His voice broke, and he turned in her arms and anchored her head in his trembling hands and locked his mouth to hers in a kiss so filled with pain and desperation that she had no choice but to hold him, to press him against her body, to kiss him back.

'It's OK,' she murmured through her kisses. 'It's OK.'

'I need you,' he said raggedly, tugging at her clothes. She stripped them off and fell with him to the bed, kissing him, stroking him, trying to heal whatever it was that had broken inside him.

His hands were frenzied, racing over her, seeking her warmth, her comfort. He moved over her, burying himself in her, his body driving into hers again and again until he stiffened and cried out, a harsh, animal sound that tore open her heart.

'Oh, Ben,' she whispered silently. 'Oh, my love...'

A sob shuddered through him, but he wrenched himself away out of her arms, jackknifing off the bed and opening drawers, pulling out underwear, a shirt, jeans, dragging them on while she lay there, her hand pressed to her mouth, and watched him helplessly with fear in her heart.

'Ben?'

'No. For God's sake, Meg, leave it.'

But she wouldn't give up, not this time. She couldn't, for his sake and for hers. She knelt up on the bed and reached for his shirt as he did, stopping him.

'Tell me,' she pleaded. 'What happened, Ben? Who was it? Who was it you couldn't save?'

He paused, his hands knotting in his shirt. For an age she thought he wouldn't answer, but then he lifted his head and looked at her, his eyes ravaged with grief.

'My son,' he said, his voice tortured. 'It was my son.'

*   *   *

'We'd been at the cottage for a few days.'

'Cottage?' Meg asked, wanting to get it clear because she knew she would only hear this once.

'In Norfolk, in a little fishing village, right on the quay with a wonderful view over the marshes and out to sea. It was tiny, just a little brick and flint terraced cottage, but it was our haven, our retreat from the hell of the East End. It was easy to get to up the M11, only a couple of hours door to door, and we loved it.'

He stared down into his tea, and Meg waited, giving him time, letting him sift through the images that were pouring through his mind as she studied him, her heart aching.

They were sitting across from each other at the table in the little living room. She'd pulled on her clothes and made tea and found a packet of biscuits and put them on the table. She pushed them towards him now, but he shook his head and carried on, his voice calm and curiously lifeless.

'Linda and Toby had been there since Wednesday. I went up on the train on Friday night, and I was going to drive them back down on Sunday, but Toby'd made friends with the little boy next door and he'd been invited round to a party on Sunday afternoon. So I caught the train, and Linda drove back on Monday.'

He paused, his eyes blank. 'I was called down to A and E on Monday afternoon. A child had been airlifted in following a crash on the M11. It happened all the time. I didn't think—not until I was in there. They were talking about the accident, about ID. Someone said the female driver was dead. The child needed intubating— he'd got facial injuries and an obstructed airway, and it needed a specialist paediatric anaesthetist to do it.

'Everything was ready, and he was lying there, a mass of tubes and wires. They'd stripped him of everything except a Mickey Mouse plaster on one scuffed, scabby little knee.' He swallowed convulsively, the only sign of emotion. 'I'd stuck it on the day before, when he'd fallen in the garden. It was the only way I could recognise him.'

Meg felt the tears well in her eyes, but she said nothing, just sat with her hands locked around her mug and waited while he carried on.

'Someone handed me a laryngoscope, and I took it, but my hand was shaking so badly I dropped it. They were still talking about ID, and I told them his name was Toby. Toby Maguire. And then he arrested, while I stood there and did nothing, and they couldn't get the tube in, and there was nothing I could do to save him. I stood there, Meg, and I watched my son die, and I did nothing.'

She gulped and scrubbed away the tears. 'You couldn't. How could you? No one would expect you—'

'He was my son!' he rasped, getting up and crossing the room in a stride, bracing himself on the window frame, staring sightlessly down the garden. 'He was my son,' he echoed, 'and I let him die.' He turned back to her. 'That's why I gave up medicine—why I can't bear to hear it, the hisses and bleeps and doors crashing open and the smell of blood. Why I didn't want to go back into a hospital to make this stupid damned programme.'

He came back to the table and sat down, cradling his mug in his hands, staring at it. He took a sip and set it down again as if he couldn't quite work out what it was for. 'At the inquest the driver in the car behind said Toby had been running up and down the back seat, and

Linda had turned round repeatedly to him. Then she turned for just too long, and the car swerved and hit a bridge support. She was killed instantly—her and the baby. She was four months pregnant.'

Meg pressed her hand to her mouth, her heart breaking for him. So much pain, so much loss. The tears flooded over again and ran unchecked down her face, but she didn't even notice. When that child had been brought in injured after the minor shunt on the school run and he'd been so angry—that was why. Because the child had been unrestrained, like Toby. And she'd asked him if he had children, and he'd said no, and so she'd told him not to be so quick to judge. Dear God. If only she'd known...

'So now you know,' he said, looking up and giving her a twisted smile. He lifted his hand and brushed her tears away with his thumb, but they fell still, an endless river, and she closed her eyes.

'Ben, I'm so sorry,' she whispered.

She heard him get up and come round behind her, patting her shoulder awkwardly. 'Don't cry. Not for me. I don't deserve it.'

She put her hand on his, gripping it, but he pulled away, distancing himself again.

'Anyway, that's it, my sorry little tale. Over years ago. Finished.'

'Is it?' she asked, turning round to face him, knowing he was shutting down again and so afraid for him. 'Are you sure? Because I don't think it's finished—not by a long way.'

'Of course it is. I failed him. What more is there to say?'

She took a deep breath and put aside her feelings,

dredging up the nurse in her and not the woman—the woman who loved him with all her heart.

'What were his injuries?'

He frowned, then shrugged. 'Brain contusions, facial fractures, abdominal and chest injuries—I don't know. All sorts.'

'What did he die of? Specifically?'

'A ruptured spleen. He bled out. But if I'd done it— if I'd intubated him instead of falling apart, he would have been on his way to Theatre. They could have saved him...'

'Could they? Ben, be realistic,' she said gently. 'Your son had massive multiple trauma. He was dead before they brought him in. It was just a matter of time.'

He shook his head. 'I should have insisted they come back on Sunday night with me. Then I would have been driving, and it wouldn't have happened.'

'You couldn't know that.'

'I could. He was naughty with her—wouldn't stay in his baby seat.'

'So she should have made him—should have pulled over and not gone on until he was back in it. Ben, it was an accident. Linda was a full-grown woman. She made a mistake, and she paid for it with her life. It wasn't Toby's fault, he was just a baby, and it certainly wasn't yours.'

'You weren't there. You didn't see it.'

'No—but I have seen it, over and over again. I saw it today, Ben, and so did you—only this time you could do something, and you did. Daniel Bright's alive because of you—because you used your skill to save him in incredibly difficult conditions.'

'Fluke.'

'Rubbish. I saw you working. You're competent, highly skilled, efficient—'

'And scared spitless. I threw up, for God's sake!'

'And who could blame you? It was all far too close to home—too hard for anyone to handle. But you did it, and you saved him. And you were wonderful with Adam. Ben, you're a good doctor, a brilliant doctor. You just have to forgive yourself.'

He turned away, his jaw working. 'Meg, leave it. I don't want to talk about it any more.'

'So what are you going to do, Ben? Bury it? Bury it again and forget it, like you have for the past however many years?'

'Five,' he said, his voice hollow. 'It's five years next week. And I don't know what I'm going to do. I just know I need you.'

Meg swallowed, praying for courage, because this was the hardest thing she'd ever had to do in her life.

'I need you, too, but you aren't free, Ben. Not to love me. And I won't settle for half of you because the other half doesn't feel, can't cry or grieve or love again. I'm not interested in an affair with you, drifting along, pretending it's all right when you're falling apart inside. I want all of it—and until you're free, you're no use to me and no use to yourself.'

He stared at her, his brow furrowed with confusion. 'But...Meg, we're so good together...'

'Are we? You won't talk to me about the things that hurt you most, Ben, and, worse still, you won't even think about them and come to terms with them. You have to learn to forgive—to forgive Toby, for getting out of his seat, and Linda, for turning round and taking her eyes off the road for too long. And you have to forgive yourself for being human, for not being able to work miracles all the time. And you have to let them go.'

'And then?'

Her voice gentled. 'Then I'll be waiting for you. I love you, Ben, and I think we could have something wonderful, but you have to go and sort yourself out, and when you have, when you've got your head on straight and your heart's healed, then come back to me. I'll be waiting.'

And then, because she couldn't stand there any longer without falling apart, because she couldn't watch him suffer any more, she turned and ran blindly down the stairs.

Fliss met her at the bottom, catching her in her arms and leading her into the sitting room, holding her while she let out all the pain and anguish in her heart, and then later, as she watched the taillights of Ben's car disappear down the drive and out of her life, she held her again, rocking and shushing her.

Tom came and went, putting the children to bed, she supposed, and with a small, still-working part of her mind she wondered how he'd got home.

'You're staying here tonight,' Fliss told her. 'I've made up a bed.'

'I'll have Ben's,' she said, needing to be near him in the only way she could, and as she lay in it later the tears welled up again, but this time she was afraid.

She'd sent him away. She'd had to, for his sake, but she was so very afraid for him, and she had no idea if she'd ever see him again...

CHAPTER TEN

IT WASN'T a conscious decision.

Ben didn't know where he was going, just that he had to get away, but then he found himself pulling up outside the cottage he hadn't seen in five long, agonisingly empty years.

The key was still on his key-ring, and with a curious sense of rightness, he climbed out of the car, walked slowly up to the door and let himself in.

It could have been yesterday.

He reached for the light switch, knowing as he did so that after five years it would be futile, but puzzlingly light flooded the room.

Oh, God. A basket of toys, a shelf of story-books, a pile of videos neatly stacked by the television. He wandered through the room, picking things up, putting them down, remembering. He almost expected them to come back in at any moment, Linda with her hair whipped every which way by the wind, Toby laughing and running to him, arms outstretched for his father's love.

But he wasn't coming back.

No. Don't think about it.

He went through into the kitchen, and found the fridge empty and the door ajar, the washing-up bowl upturned in the sink, three pairs of wellies lined up by the back door under their coats, all of it neat and tidy and on hold until the next visit.

It was like Goldilocks and the three bears.

He went upstairs, into the bedroom he'd shared with

Linda, but it was empty, the bed stripped, the quilt neatly folded over the blanket box at the end. There was nothing there to evoke a memory, nothing to tear at him.

Maybe there was nothing left inside him after all.

He left the room and crossed the landing, then stopped. Such a little bed, with its colourful bedding and a tired, sad little teddy on the pillow, abandoned and all alone for the past five years.

How stupid, that something so small could be the thing that broke him. He lifted it with infinite tenderness, sat down on the bed with it in his hands, and wept.

'Are you sure you're up to this?'

Meg nodded. Tom was being so kind, so solicitous, but she needed to get back to reality. She'd spent enough days lying in Ben's sheets indulging in her endless tears.

'It was only a week, after all. I can't let it change my life,' she said, trying to smile, but Tom just shook his head.

'A week, a year, a moment—it doesn't matter how long it is. When you know something, you know it. I knew with Felicity the instant I saw her.'

She sucked in a huge breath. 'I can't get hold of him, Tom,' she said, her voice full of fear for him. 'His mobile must be switched off, and he's not answering his emails. Pete can't get hold of him either, and keeps ringing me to see if I've contacted him—not that I'd tell him if I did.'

'No. I don't think Ben needs him at the moment.'

'I don't think he ever did.'

'I don't know. The programme might have been good

for him in a way. It gave him time to draw breath, to get a little distance. He must have needed that.'

'Can you try and contact him?' she asked. 'You might have some idea—'

'Meg, I haven't. I lost contact with him years ago, and if it hadn't been for this coincidence I probably would never have seen him again. I have no idea where he could be. If I did, I'd tell you, you know that. I'm sure he'll be all right. He needs to be alone, to deal with this.'

She nodded, knowing it was true but still afraid for him, needing the reassurance of his voice. 'He might contact you,' she said, clutching at straws.

'He might. Any message?'

'Only that I love him. Crazy, isn't it?'

'I don't think so. I love him, too. He's a good man, and he's been through hell. Still going through it. Give him time. He'll be back.'

Meg sighed. 'I wish I had your confidence,' she said softly. 'Right. I need to go and find Angie. I hope we're busy today.'

'I don't doubt it. The week's been hellish so far, don't see why today should be any different. Oh, by the way, Mrs Bright's been asking to see you. She wanted to thank you for all you did on Sunday.'

Meg swallowed. She wasn't sure she wanted to be reminded of the RTA that had pushed Ben over the edge, but she wanted to know how the whole family were, and if she should manage to contact Ben, she wanted to be able to tell him that they were on the mend.

'I'll go up and see her later. Is she still in Maternity?'

Tom shook his head. 'No, they've discharged her.

She's in Paeds with Daniel and Adam, and her husband's in Orthopaedics.'

'OK. I'll find her later. Must go, Angie will think I've abandoned her.'

Angie didn't. Angie thought she was mad to have come back, and put her on Triage where she wouldn't face anything too traumatic and would have plenty to keep her occupied.

She went up to see the Bright family in her afternoon break, and found them all clustered round Daniel's bed. The swelling in his throat had subsided now and he was fully conscious and looking pretty good, considering. His mother was sitting by the bed with Adam cradled asleep on her lap, and apart from the huge bruise down the left side of her face where she'd smashed against the side window, she looked remarkably good.

And Mr Bright was there in a neck collar, his right foot in a cast supported on a slide-out board attached to his wheelchair, enjoying a brief visit to his family. He still looked a little rough and he wasn't able to turn his head to see her, but, all things considered, Meg thought, they looked pretty darned good.

'Meg,' Mrs Bright said, reaching out a hand, and Meg took it and squeezed it hard, bending over to drop a kiss on her cheek.

'Hi. Good to see you looking so well, all of you. How's it going, Daniel?'

'OK. Throat's sore,' he said in a gruff little voice. 'And I'm bored.'

She smiled. 'I'm sure. You'll be up and about in no time, though, I imagine.'

'He's got a cracked tibia, but otherwise he's fine, apart from the throat and some bruised ribs,' Mr Bright put in. 'They expect us all to make a full recovery.'

'Thanks to you and Ben Maguire,' his wife added. 'I didn't know he was a doctor.'

Meg felt her heart twist. 'Yes. He's left medicine, but he's still a doctor at heart.'

Dear Lord, how could she talk about him, smile and laugh with the family, accept their thanks, promise to pass on their messages to Ben, when all the while she had no idea where he was or if he'd ever come back?

She escaped as soon as she could, arriving back in A and E to the news that her flat had been broken into and ransacked.

It was the last straw.

Angie, supportive as ever, sent her home to talk to the police, and she walked into a scene of devastation.

She knew who it was, of course. They'd made the mistake of scrawling 'Bitch' on her bathroom mirror in lipstick, and the only thing missing was her phone.

'Do you reckon it was the same gang?'

'Oh, yes,' she said with a tearful sigh. 'They've had it in for me for ages.'

'He was released on bail, you know—the lad who hit you.'

Meg shook her head. He should have been locked up. Oh, well, at least Ben wasn't here to see it.

She went to phone Fliss, but the handset on her house phone was smashed, so as soon as the police had finished she packed up a few things and drove round to see her.

'You've got to move out of there,' Fliss said instantly, pushing Meg into a kitchen chair and plonking tea down in front of her. 'It's too dangerous. I didn't want you to go back there after your car was vandalised. I should have said something. Still, at least you weren't hurt this time.'

'It's trashed,' she said, and felt the tears prickle again. 'I know it was nothing special, but it was home, and they've trashed it completely. All my things…'

'Come here. We've got the flat going begging. Have that.'

Meg shook her head, horribly tempted. 'I can't. I don't want to invade your privacy.'

Fliss threw back her head and laughed. 'Privacy? What's that? We live with Tom's parents and five children. We don't *have* privacy.'

'Well, you should.'

'We do. At night. That's enough. Too much, in fact. I seem to be pregnant again.'

Meg forgot her troubles instantly. 'Fliss! That's wonderful!'

'Is it? Six children?'

'You love it,' Meg reminded her, and she laughed.

'Keep telling me that. I'm going to have to buy an industrial washing machine and dishwasher, I think. It's a good job the Aga's got four ovens or I'd be pressing the old range into service.'

'Does Tom know?'

She nodded. 'He was there this morning when I did the test.' She gave a wry smile. 'We got a little careless last Sunday—we'd had you and Ben round and had quite a bit to drink, and we just…' She shrugged. 'I didn't really worry because I'm still breast-feeding, but I had this sudden wave of nausea and exhaustion, and I still had the other test from last time—it was a twin pack, and I thought it might be out of date. But…well, apparently not.'

'And what did he say?'

'Tom?' She smiled. 'He just grinned and hugged me.'

'A bit of an improvement on last time, then.'

'Oh, yes. But, then, we are married now, and he knows I love his kids to bits. But never mind about me. As I say, we don't need privacy, and if I'm going to feel awful I won't worry about making use of you to help with the kids when I'm feeling rough.'

'You don't need to feel awful anyway—Fliss, are you sure? You ought to ask Tom.'

'He's already been on the phone. He told me not to let you say no.'

She bit her lip, suddenly overcome by their incredible kindness.

'I'll pay rent,' she insisted, and Fliss opened her mouth, then closed it again.

'OK. If you must. A little. And I'll pay you for babysitting.'

'You will not. And it's only temporary, till I find somewhere else.' She sighed. 'I'll have to get a little van to move my stuff— What?'

Fliss was laughing. 'We've got a people carrier, idiot. We can take the seats out and fit all your stuff in it with room to spare. Tom said he'd do it tonight. You aren't to go back there alone.'

Meg nodded. She'd been worrying about that, and since her flat was completely trashed and it was furnished anyway, her next move was to phone her landlord with the news. And later that night, with the remains of her life safely installed into Ben's flat— strange, how she thought of it as his—she sat down on the little sofa and faced the reality of her future.

She had no home, the man she'd given her heart to for ever was out of reach, and if it hadn't been for Fliss and Tom, she would have been truly homeless.

Instead, she was living in their house, surrounded by the bustle and clatter of family life, the laughter and contentment all around evidence of their deep and abiding love for each other, only serving to underline just how alone she really was.

'Ben, where are you?' she murmured. 'Are you all right? I love you. Take care. Come home to me soon, my love.'

Come home…

It was finished.

Ben stood back and looked around, and gave a slow nod. Good. It was all fresh now, clean and light and airy, the kitchen and bathroom refitted, the house repainted from end to end, inside and out. And the garden was looking wonderful, thanks in no small part to Margaret, his next-door neighbour.

For the last five years, unbeknown to him, she and his parents had kept an eye on the place, waiting for the time when he would return.

And now it was time to go.

The estate agent had been that morning, valued it and put a sign in the little front garden, and already he had three people lined up to view.

Ben's job was done. With one last backward glance, he closed the door behind him, got into the car and drove off. Back to London, to face the mayhem created by his walk-out.

He had no idea what Pete had been doing for the past four months. He just knew he'd got sick of the constant calls he'd refused to answer and chucked his phone into the sea one day. Better than switching it off and then checking it every few minutes to see if Meg had rung. Of course she hadn't. She'd sent him away, and rightly. She wouldn't contact him.

So it hadn't mattered that he didn't have a phone.

Now, though, it did matter, and so he went back to London, found Pete and endured the haranguing for the last time, put together a final edit on the last programme and met up with Steve for lunch at the end of the second week.

'So—how are you? Really?' Steve asked after the preliminaries, his eyes concerned.

'I'm OK. Getting there. I just wanted to thank you for everything you've done with me for the past three years.'

Steve smiled. 'It's been a pleasure. You've been interesting to work with—entertaining, watching you and Pete hammer it out day by day.'

Ben gave a short huff of laughter. 'Interesting? You reckon? Still, it's all over now. He tells me you've left, too?'

'Yes.' A nod, a slow smile. 'I'm going to be working with Lena Murray.'

Ben's eyes narrowed. 'Lena? The war correspondent?'

'You know quite well who I mean.'

He felt the slow smile spread over his face. 'Well, well. So what about Susie?'

Steve shrugged. 'Susie's history. We've been going nowhere for ages. And Lena phoned me, after the award thing. She saw us on the television, rang for a chat, and I finally plucked up the courage to tell her how I feel.'

'And?'

He smiled. 'She feels the same. I'm off with her in a couple of days. We're going to be filming in Africa. And for the first time in ages, I'm looking forward to it.' He stirred his coffee idly, then looked up at Ben, his eyes keen. 'So what are you doing about Meg?'

*   *   *

'I've had a phone call.'

'Who from?' Meg asked, busy checking stores in Resus.

'Ben.'

Her hands stilled, her heart in her mouth. She drew in a sharp breath, then let it out slowly and turned to face Tom. 'How is he?'

'OK. He wanted to know how you were. I think he wants to see you.'

'What did you tell him?'

'That he would have to be very sure of what he wanted. That you were vulnerable, and that I'd kill him if he hurt you, either deliberately or carelessly.'

She felt her eyes fill. 'I hope that won't be necessary.'

'So do I.'

'When's he coming?' she asked, her heart skittering against her ribs.

Tom shrugged. 'I don't know. He didn't say.' He checked his watch. 'You'd better go, hadn't you, if you're meeting Fliss up at Ultrasound?'

She nodded. 'I was just finishing off. I'll take my coat—I'll go home with Fliss.'

They had to queue for ages and Fliss was fretting about picking the little ones up from school by the time they got out. She took Charlotte from Meg and tucked her into her car seat, then went home via the school.

She drove round to the back and put the car into the cart lodge, then, as Meg was helping Abby out, Fliss said her name and she looked up and saw him.

Finally.

'Will you be all right?' Fliss asked softly, and she nodded.

'Yes. I'll be fine.' She pulled her coat closer, wrapping her arms across her chest, holding her elbows to steady the sudden trembling in her body.

Fliss ushered the children away, and after an endless pause Ben walked slowly towards her, his face unsmiling.

'Hi.'

'Hi. Tom said you rang.'

'Did he tell you he threatened to kill me?'

She laughed softly, and it broke the ice. His face relaxed and his mouth quirked into a smile. 'I've missed you,' he confessed. 'Are you all right?'

'I'm fine. What about you?'

His eyes scanned her face—looking for clues?—and he nodded thoughtfully. 'I'm OK. I'll do.' He looked around, then back to her. 'Can we go somewhere to talk?'

'The flat? I'm living there now. My flat in town was turned over by those little scallies.'

His mouth flattened. 'I wondered why you weren't there any more. Were you all right?'

'Fine. I was at work. Fliss and Tom wouldn't let me stay there, though.'

'Sounds like them.'

She led the way, going in through her own door on the side and up the stairs on legs like jelly. Was he really all right? And would he still want her? They weren't one and the same thing, necessarily...

'Tea?'

He looked around him, his face unsmiling, deep in thought.

She put the kettle on anyway, and turned up the heating. It was chilly in the flat at the end of the day, and she kept her coat on. The kettle boiled, she made tea in mugs and put them down on the table, sitting down and sliding a mug towards him. 'Biscuit?'

'Um…no, thanks.' He took the chair opposite her, and she suddenly realised he was nervous. Crazily, that made her feel better. More hopeful.

He fiddled with his mug, pushed it around, lined up the handle with a pen that was lying on the table. Then finally he looked up and met her eyes.

'I…ah…I wanted to thank you. You were right, I was a mess. I was running away, hiding from a reality I couldn't deal with.'

'And now?'

His smile was bleak. 'I'm getting there. Done a lot of forgiving—Linda for having the accident, Toby for causing it, me for not saving Toby when, as you rightly said, he was unsavable. And I grieved. You were right about that, too. I hadn't grieved, hadn't let them go, hadn't said goodbye. There was a huge chunk of me set in ice, and you started the thaw. I just had to go and sit it out.'

'And now?' she asked, hardly daring to breathe.

'Now I've come back. I've sold the house in Norfolk, put my flat in London on the market and finished the final edit on the programme. I'm free to move on—and my heart, for what it's worth, is about as healed as it's going to get. We aren't meant to lose our children, and there'll always be a part of me that belongs to Toby. There's nothing I can do about that, but the rest of me— if you want it—is yours.'

His face blurred, and she blinked, the joy in her heart threatening to spill over into tears. 'I said I'd be here for you. I said I'd wait.'

'But five months? I had no idea it would take so long, but I just had to work through it.'

'I tried to contact you. Your phone was never on.'

'I threw it in the sea. Pete was driving me crazy.'

She nodded. 'I can understand that. I feel sorry for the people who nicked my phone.'

His mouth quirked. 'I don't. Poetic justice.'

He paused, then put his hand into his pocket and drew it out again. 'You said when we were down in London, before the award thing, that you had no use for jewellery, but there is one thing that I feel you really ought to have, if you can cope with it. It comes with a hell of a lot of strings attached, mind you, but it also comes with all my love. And I know I said a part of me belonged to Toby, but I'd like to share that part with you, because I think you understand.'

He lifted his hand and held it out flat, palm up, and she felt her breath jam in her throat. 'Oh, Ben, it's beautiful!'

'It's not a solitaire. I know everybody wants one, but they always seem so impractical, sticking up in the way, and this one just seemed to be you.'

She reached out a trembling hand to touch it, a band set with five perfect, flawless stones. 'Put it on,' he said, but she shook her head.

'Not yet. I've got something to show you first— something you need to see.'

She delved into her bag and came up with the photo, sliding it across the table to him. He set the ring down and took the photo, picking it up and smiling. He looked a little bemused.

'The 3-D scanner you were sponsored for. Good grief, it's so real. Beautiful. Amazing. Fliss and Tom's baby, I take it. He said they were having another.'

She shook her head. 'No. It's not Fliss and Tom's. It's ours. She…is ours.'

His mouth opened, and he sucked in a huge breath, his eyes locked with hers. 'Ours?' he whispered soundlessly, and stared down at the picture of his child. 'Meg—how? When?'

'That Sunday evening, after the accident. I followed you back here. You needed me. I didn't think. It didn't matter. Only you mattered.'

'And this—she—is the result?'

Meg nodded. 'So, now you know, I come with quite a lot of strings myself.'

He set the photo down with a hand that shook, and picked up the ring. 'Well matched, then,' he said, his voice as unsteady as his hand. 'So will you take it? As a symbol of my love?'

She couldn't speak. She just bit her lips and nodded, and he slipped it onto her ring finger and held it there, his eyes locked on hers. For a moment, he glanced down at the picture of his daughter, then looked back at Meg, and his eyes were filled with tears. 'I love you,' he said quietly. 'Marry me, Meg. Soon.'

'Very soon. As soon as you like. But first I need a hug,' she said, and then she was in his arms, and he was laughing and crying and holding her close.

'I've missed you,' he said softly. 'Missed you so much, but I had to be sure it was right. I didn't want to short-change you.'

'You haven't. You couldn't. Just to know you is more than enough reward. I love you, Ben.' She kissed him tenderly. 'I love you.'

'One thing I forgot,' he said, lying beside her in the bed, his hand gently curved over his baby daughter. 'Tom told me there was a job at the hospital. They're looking for a paediatric anaesthetist to work in pain management. It's a pretty tough thing to spend your life doing, but you can make a real difference, and I really don't want to go back to emergency work. I know I can do it, but I don't want to be faced with it day after day. It's still raw, and I guess it always will be, but pain management's been a bit of a hobby of mine for a while, and I've done some reading up. I'm going to go and have a chat to them, see if they'll take me on perhaps as a locum.'

'So you'd be working here?'

'If I get it.'

'Are you sure? About going back into medicine? Don't do it for me, Ben. You need to do it for you.'

'I am. I've missed it—missed it ridiculously badly. Missed having a purpose, missed being needed, missed the challenge and the technical difficulties and the teamwork—all of it. And if it hadn't been for you, I might never have realised.'

'If it hadn't been for Pete, we would never have met. Now, there's a thought!'

He groaned and kissed her. 'Don't ask me to thank him. That would be a step too far.'

She laughed and kissed him back. 'I don't think he deserves it. We might have to invite him to the wedding—and Steve.'

'Steve's in Africa with Lena Murray, the war correspondent.'

Her eyes widened. 'Really?'

'Really. She's his type.'

'Not yours?'

'Not mine. You're mine.'

'What—bossy and inquisitive and never knowing when to back off?'

'I love you,' he said with a grin. 'You can't be that

bad. That's criticising my judgement. You wouldn't want to do that.'

'Of course not,' she said with a chuckle, then she frowned. 'Talking of inviting people to the wedding, we ought to go and tell Fliss and Tom and put them out of their misery.'

He smiled and drew her closer. 'Later,' he said. 'If I know Tom, he's got a vintage champagne on ice by now. It needs time to chill and, frankly, after the last few months, so do I, so come here and let me hold you.'

She went willingly, snuggling into his arms and falling asleep while his fingers curved protectively over his tiny daughter, feeling her stretch and kick beneath his hand.

A new beginning, a future, better than he could ever have dared to dream.

Ben closed his eyes, drew Meg closer still and watched over them while she slept...

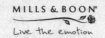

LOGAN'S LEGACY

*Because birthright has its privileges and
family ties run deep*

FREE

4 BOOKS AND A SURPRISE GIFT!

We would like to take this opportunity to thank you for reading this Mills & Boon® book by offering you the chance to take FOUR more specially selected titles from the Medical Romance™ series absolutely FREE! We're also making this offer to introduce you to the benefits of the Reader Service™—

- ★ **FREE home delivery**
- ★ **FREE gifts and competitions**
- ★ **FREE monthly Newsletter**
- ★ **Books available before they're in the shops**
- ★ **Exclusive Reader Service offers**

Accepting these FREE books and gift places you under no obligation to buy; you may cancel at any time, even after receiving your free shipment. Simply complete your details below and return the entire page to the address below. You don't even need a stamp!

YES! Please send me 4 free Medical Romance books and a surprise gift. I understand that unless you hear from me, I will receive 6 superb new titles every month for just £2.75 each, postage and packing free. I am under no obligation to purchase any books and may cancel my subscription at any time. The free books and gift will be mine to keep in any case.

M5ZEE

Ms/Mrs/Miss/Mr...Initials ....
BLOCK CAPITALS PLEASE

Surname ....

Address ....

....

....Postcode ....

Send this whole page to:
The Reader Service, FREEPOST CN81, Croydon, CR9 3WZ